BROKEN VOWS

Stephanie Daniels

ZEBRA BOOKS
KENSINGTON PUBLISHING CORP.

*With love to my mother and father,
who nurtured my creativity, and to
my husband, Chris, who believed in
me before I believed in myself.*

ZEBRA BOOKS are published by

Kensington Publishing Corp.
850 Third Avenue
New York, NY 10022

Copyright © 1996 by Stephanie Quinn Westphal

Zebra and the Z logo Reg. U.S. Pat. & TM Off.

First Zebra Printing: June, 1996
10 9 8 7 6 5 4 3 2 1

Printed in the United States of America

One

"Hey, sexy mama, take me for a ride!" The voice was low and suggestive.

Wendy Valdez' head whipped sideways toward the speaker, who was leaning in the passenger window of her van. A skinny teenage boy stared back, raised finely arched eyebrows above caramel-colored eyes, and gave her a disturbingly adult once-over.

Wendy glanced at the address on the piece of paper in her hand, then checked the numbers above the door of the shabby building that loomed up behind the boy. Yep, this had to be Valencia House, a shelter for runaway teenagers. And this kid with the knowing brown eyes was probably one of the youths she wanted to help. Only what his eyes were suggesting wasn't exactly the kind of help she'd had in mind.

"What ya say?" The boy readjusted the hairnet that covered his dark, wavy locks. "You game or what?"

"No, I'm definitely *not* game." She forced her voice to remain calm; she wasn't about to give in to the ripple of fear that moved through her. After all, he was only a kid acting tough—even if he did look as though he'd seen more action in fifteen years than she'd seen in twenty-nine. She rolled up the window.

Turning off the ignition, she took her purse—there was no point in tempting fate—and stepped out into the brisk wind that blew off the San Francisco Bay.

"Are you from the shelter?"

"I'm ready to shelter you anytime, sweet thing."

Before Wendy could think of a response, the front doors of the building flew open and a large, forceful-looking man burst out. About thirty years old, he had a shock of black hair and the bluest eyes she'd ever seen. Sunlight glinted off his high cheekbones and the strong lines of his jaw.

"Lamar!" the man barked. "You can run, but you can't hide."

"I . . . I was just gettin' some fresh air." The young boy backed away slowly from the man.

Watching the stranger, Wendy had to admit that he was attractive—if you were drawn to bearlike men. Since she was only five feet four, she preferred men of average height and build who didn't dwarf her. This man had to be six foot three or four, with muscles that made him look as if he filled his spare hours by pulling tractors with his bare hands. Or perhaps his teeth.

"Get your rear inside." With one powerful hand, the man who must be Lamar's teacher spun him toward the shelter door. "The computer's free, and you're next on the sign-up sheet."

"All *right!*" the teenager said, his eyes lighting up. "My turn to check out the new flight simulator." He intercepted the man's stern look. "Don't say it, boss. 'You gotta pay before you play.' I'll do my English paper first." He dashed inside the building.

Wendy found herself standing on the sidewalk, staring up at the towering stranger.

Turning his midnight blue gaze on her, he asked, "Can I help you with something?"

Suddenly she felt unnerved. Now that he was addressing her instead of Lamar, his voice was smooth and well modulated. An uncomfortable wave of heat moved across her cheeks. Surprised, she tried to remember the last time she'd blushed. "I'm Wendy Valdez." She extended her hand. "And I—"

"Great! The woman donating the computer desks." He gripped her fingers in a firm handshake. "Jack O'Connor. Pleased to meet you." When he smiled, he looked almost warm and approachable. "We've been waiting with bated breath ever since we got your call."

"Really?" She hadn't thought her donation was such a big deal.

"You bet. I strong-armed Apple into donating a few computers, then we didn't have anywhere to put them. We jerry-built some old tables—just as a temporary solution—until we could find real desks."

She could just imagine this dynamic guy talking corporations out of computers and unwary women out of other things. "Glad I could help."

"Let's see what you brought."

She opened the back doors of her van. Inside were six unconventionally shaped chairs and computer desks decorated in neon yellow, orange, pink, and purple. She'd spent painstaking hours designing, building, then painting the pieces herself. Over the past two years, she'd struggled to establish herself as an independent furniture maker. Now her work was beginning to make a name for her among local interior designers who relied on an original "Valdez" to complete the modern look in a particular room.

Running her hand over the back of one of the chairs, she said proudly, "Here they are."

A look of almost comical dismay came over Jack's face. "These are the desks?"

This wasn't the first time she'd encountered this kind of reaction. Even her own mother didn't "get" her furniture. Apparently Mr. O'Connor wasn't someone who appreciated the avant-garde. "You sound less than thrilled."

"No, no, don't get me wrong." Repressing what might have been a smile, he cleared his throat. "We appreciate all donations. It's just that we've, uh, no one's ever given us anything quite as . . . distinctive as this."

"Distinctive?"

"That's right."

"I'll take that as a compliment."

"Please do." A glimmer appeared in his eyes, then vanished. "I'll get some of the boys to bring in your furniture. Come with me." Effortlessly hoisting a desk up on his shoulder, he turned toward the shelter. "Oh, and lock your car. This isn't the best neighborhood for a woman alone."

"You've had problems here?" she asked. When he shifted the desk, she could see his biceps flexing beneath his charcoal gray sweatshirt.

"Four tape decks stolen from my car in the last two years. Now I hum to myself while I drive."

After securing the van, she followed him through large wooden doors at the front of the building and into a freshly painted hallway. As she hurried to catch up with him, she noticed that his posture was excellent—almost too good. On the other hand, the man had great buns. Had he trained in the military or something?

Wendy usually steered clear of highly disciplined men; not only did they remind her of her dad, but they hardly ever liked the things that made life worthwhile to her: art, music, dance, or curling up in front of the VCR on a Friday night with a British spy movie and a big bowl of popcorn.

When he came to an abrupt stop outside a door, she almost slammed into him.

After lowering her desk to the hallway floor, he opened the door and nodded for her to precede him. "Let me show you how much we need your donation."

Inside the clean, well-lit room, a dozen teenagers hunched over work stations, unaware of their visitors. Several state-of-the-art computers were bolted respectively to recycled school desks, a contraption made out of two wobbly-looking coffee tables, and a sewing table minus the Singer.

She shook her head in wonder. "You weren't kidding when you said you needed work desks."

"Yep. We get plenty of chances to find out why necessity is the mother of invention."

She smiled at his ingenuity until it dawned on her that her own hand-tooled furniture would soon get the same harsh treatment. She told herself to relax; she had to give her gift, then let it go. In Brazil she'd learned that painful lesson when she tried to teach the farmers why it was better to save the rain forests than to graze cattle for fast-food burgers.

As she looked around, she mentally rearranged the space: her desks against one wall, a long worktable on the other, better lighting, a sofa in the corner, and . . . She stopped herself. Her goal today was to drop off her furniture, not redesign the shelter. She'd probably never see this room again anyway, so what difference did it make?

A boy with slicked-back ebony hair glanced up at her, then let out a wolf whistle. "Mamacita!"

Jack glared at the offending teenager. "When I bring a lady into the room, I expect you to show her respect."

The young man clenched his fists, then shrugged. "All right, boss." Giving a quick bow in her direction, he said, "Sorry, ma'am. Pleased to meet ya."

She could only guess what the teenager's apology must have cost him. "I'm pleased to meet you, too."

"Time's wasting," Jack said. "Everybody get back to work."

As the kids reluctantly turned to face their computers, she noticed that they all wore clean, pressed blue jeans and white shirts. She had expected them to be decked out in typical street garb. Their uniformity disappeared above the collar, however. A smile twitched at her lips as she noted a pretty girl with a retro-sixties beehive hairstyle, a tall, gangly boy whose long, limp bangs made him resemble a sheepdog, and a girl who looked as if she'd styled her straw-blond curls with industrial-strength glue and an eggbeater. Lamar sat at a desk in the corner, vainly patting his hairnet in between bouts of typing on a keyboard.

She said softly to Jack, "I'm impressed that you got them to wear uniforms."

"Only took a few battles."

"You're smart to let them express themselves in their hairstyles."

"Makes them feel they've got control over some part of their lives—and they need that. If they feel trapped, they run." His expression softened as he regarded his students. "I keep them in line, but I make sure not to rein them in too tightly."

"Sounds like a wise policy."

"The bottom line is, I want my kids to feel like winners."

As she studied the teenagers' faces, hardened beyond their years, she detected something wild and barely restrained about them; after all, they'd had to survive on the streets. At the same time, she sensed a heartbreaking fragility behind their tough masks. What careful handling these teens must need, she thought. Her admiration for Jack edged up a few notches.

"Mr. O'Connor," one of the kids said. "I can't figure out this math program. Can you help me?"

"Do you mind?" Jack looked at her. "It'll just take a minute."

"No. Go right ahead."

Kneeling his large frame next to the boy, he patiently talked him through an equation on the computer screen. "That's all it takes. You try it."

Tentatively the boy tapped on a few keys. The screen flashed a graphic of a hand with the thumb up in the victory sign. "All right! Now I get it."

Silently Wendy watched the interchange between the two, noting that the respect went both ways. She felt a lump in her throat and squeezed her eyes shut tightly for a moment. Jeez, why did she have to go all soft whenever she saw an authority figure taking the time to find out what was really bugging a kid?

"Good going, Ralphie." Jack ruffled the boy's hair, then turned to the other kids. "Lamar, D.J., Reynaldo. Come with me. I need your help unloading some furniture Ms. Valdez kindly donated."

"You got it, Mr. O'Connor," said Lamar.

Like a wolf pack, the rough-looking gang rose together and converged in her direction.

As the boys trooped down the hall, Jack stopped at another door and pulled it open for her. "Here's my office. Help yourself to some coffee while we bring in the furniture."

Fishing out her keys from her purse, she handed them to him. "Won't you need these?"

"Only if you want us to enter your van _legally._"

"I think that would probably be best." She kept a poker face.

"Probably. Make yourself comfortable. I'll be back in a few minutes." Then he added in a low voice so the boys couldn't hear, "If you're in the mood for something sweet, there are some M & M's in the bottom drawer of the desk. Help yourself."

"Mm, how intriguing." She hadn't figured him for the type of guy who kept a secret stash of candy.

"Leave a few for me, will you?"

"After you insulted my furniture?" She gave him her Mona Lisa smile. "I'll give it serious consideration."

"I'd appreciate that," he said, then quietly closed the door behind him.

Alone in the room, she surveyed her surroundings. Jack's massive oak desk sat in the corner, supporting neat stacks of paper, a personal computer, and a phone with several lights blinking. Shelves above the desk held books on psychology, theology, and the martial arts, as well as collections of humorous essays. She could just imagine him sitting at his personal command station, fielding crisis after crisis with the same ease he'd displayed when he carried one of her desks.

On one wall, drawings that looked as if they'd been done by the kids jockeyed for space with a homemade wooden cross and several photographs. In the photos, Jack received awards, stood at podiums, and shook hands with various San Francisco politicians. The man seemed awfully well connected for a guy running a shelter. She sensed something mysterious or hidden about him. Maybe it was the knowing look behind his smile or the intensity he covered up with his easy charm.

Looking around, she wondered if the teenagers found this office a welcome refuge from the chaos and decay outside. If she were one of them, she'd feel that this was a place where she'd get a fair shake.

At that moment, a harried-looking woman with mousy blond hair up in a bun bustled into the room. She stopped short when she saw Wendy.

"Oh, my goodness. I didn't know anyone was in here." She glanced down at the appointment book she held, then stuck out a thin, age-spotted hand. "I'm Thelma Hughes, Mr. O'Connor's assistant. You must be the woman who'll be teaching art to the students."

Wendy clasped the woman's hand, then explained she was just there to make a donation.

"Oh, that's too bad." Mrs. Hughes's features crumpled into a look of concern. "I guess Miss Mott is going to be late—if she shows up at all. Poor, dear Mr. O'Connor is having the worst time finding someone willing to teach those children. But one must have faith—as Mr. O'Connor always says. Things will turn out."

With that, the little birdlike woman darted out of the room, her tweed-covered bottom twitching back and forth like a waddling duck's behind.

So Jack was having a hard time finding a teacher. Wendy wasn't surprised. She didn't think anyone could pay her enough to tackle a houseful of needy teenagers. When she was through dropping off her furniture, she'd be happy to call it a day.

After fixing herself a cup of coffee, she took a handful of M & M's, then sat back on the comfortable couch. She was savoring the last morsel of candy when the door opened. Jack came in, then casually planted himself on the edge of his desk.

"Let me write you a receipt," he said. "For tax purposes."

At that moment, Mrs. Hughes popped her head back in the room. "Excuse me, Mr. O'Connor, but I just wanted to let you know that the applicant for the teaching position canceled her appointment." Almost as quickly as she'd appeared, his assistant vanished again.

Disappointment barely registered on Jack's stark features before he took a pad from a neat pile on his desk. In precise, bold script, he wrote out a receipt. "I'll let you fill in what you think your furniture is worth. And thanks again."

She stood and shook his hand. "My pleasure, Mr. O'Connor. What you're doing here is wonderful." As she met his intense gaze, she felt that she could trust him with a more personal thought. "You know, when I was in high school, one of the only things that got me through those horrible years was my love of art." She shrugged self-consciously. "If my furniture inspires even one kid to express his imagination a little—then I'll feel like I've really helped—"

His deep voice cut her off. "What we really need, Ms. Valdez, is someone to *work* with these kids. One on one. Someone willing to put herself on the line." His dark blue eyes bored into her, as if he were taking her measure. "You make your living as an artist. We have a part-time volunteer teaching job open. If you really want to help, why don't you teach an art class?"

His forcefulness caught her off guard. While she admired what he was doing, that didn't mean she was ready to teach here. "Now, hold on a second. I just came to make a simple donation."

"You're right. I apologize." Turning abruptly, he walked to the window that overlooked a dumpster and a few junked cars. "Not everyone can—or wants to—make an individual commitment."

For a moment, Wendy was speechless. He couldn't know it, but he'd zeroed in on one of her weak spots. She straightened in her seat. "And you don't think I can?"

He turned back. With one glance, he seemed to catalog her clothes, and her with them. Wendy was painfully aware that her raspberry sweater was the softest cashmere, her slim, black pants of one hundred percent wool, and her knee-high boots fashioned out of supple glove leather. Did he think that because she allowed herself the luxury of a few expensive clothes, she didn't have compassion for people who weren't as lucky as she was?

"Most people would rather give money or things," he said in a weary voice. "It's easier. Forgive me if I've hurt your feelings by being honest."

Scenes from her volunteer jobs in the past flashed before her eyes: the summer she'd spent teaching retarded children to swim, the six months in Calcutta when she'd helped feed starving kids, and her stint as a community organizer to save the Amazonian rain forests.

He didn't know what kind of person she was. It wasn't fair to dismiss her as someone who couldn't make a personal commitment.

"You seem to have misjudged me," she said calmly. "I hadn't thought of teaching here, but now that you've mentioned it, I think I'd like that."

He shot her a skeptical glance. "Ms. Valdez, I know I overstepped my bounds a few minutes ago. I backed you into a corner. Please don't think you have to volunteer . . ."

"I want to," she insisted. "I've done volunteer work before, and it made me feel good. What hours do you need me?"

He looked as if he didn't know whether to believe her or not. Finally he said, "The teacher was going to do a special program on Tuesday and Thursday afternoons from one to two."

"Fine." She picked up her purse. "I'll see you then. You just got yourself an art teacher."

That got him. His blue eyes widened.

With an airy wave good-bye, she headed for the door.

Two

Tuesday morning, Mrs. Hughes rapped on Jack's partially opened door, then popped her head around the corner. A big smile on her face, she announced, "Miss Valdez is back."

Surprised, Jack pushed aside the grant application he'd been writing. An image of Wendy Valdez surfaced in his mind: curly reddish-brown hair, big brown eyes, nice figure, expensive clothes. She seemed like someone who'd be comfortable at the type of trendy, overly loud restaurant that served absurdly tiny portions for an exorbitant amount of money. A well-to-do, privileged woman, who painted weird-looking chairs and every once in a while made charitable donations. Not someone who would take on the challenge of teaching runaway street kids.

He knew his comments when they'd first met had stung Wendy's pride, prompting her to volunteer to teach. But with a cynicism developed over time, he'd assumed that she'd go home, then change her mind—probably without even calling to let him know. He'd seen it happen too many times to be shocked when someone—in a moment of empathy—promised to help, then backed out once the impulse passed.

Removing his reading glasses, he rubbed his eyes. "I never thought we'd see her again."

The tiny woman closed the door behind her, whispering conspiratorially. "Didn't I tell you she'd be back?"

"You did. And you're rarely wrong, Thelma."

"Well, my daddy always said I was an excellent judge of character." She primly adjusted the bow at the neck of her blouse. "Now, don't forget you have lunch with the mayor today in . . ." Checking her watch, she exclaimed, "Oh, my goodness! I left my pineapple upside-down cake in the oven!" Without another word, she darted out the door at the back of Jack's office that led to the kitchen.

Although Mrs. Hughes didn't live at the shelter, she often baked goodies for Jack and the kids. She was a firm believer that warm cookies were directly tied to mental stability.

Jack went to the waiting room to welcome Wendy. Stopping in the doorway, he silently regarded his visitor. She'd kicked her shoes off. With her legs casually tucked up beneath her on the couch, she was engrossed in reading a magazine and hadn't noticed him. Her short skirt showed off trim, well-toned legs. His eyes moved up to her curly auburn hair, which fell across her forehead and cast shadows on her small, straight nose and soft-looking mouth.

How would it feel to kiss those pink lips? Automatically he told himself to stop thinking of her sexually, then remembered he didn't have to restrict himself that way anymore. It wasn't a sin to recognize that she was attractive.

Coughing to announce his presence, he waited to catch her eye. "Hello, Ms. Valdez. Come into my office."

"Good morning!" she said, her voice cheerful and confident. She held up a large fishing tackle box. "I've brought supplies: paint, brushes, some butcher paper. I came a few hours early so that I can get set up." After slipping on her shoes, she rose. "So where's my classroom?"

"Slow down," he said gruffly. "We've got to talk first. Want some coffee?"

"That'd be nice, thank you." She followed him into his office. Taking a seat in the overstuffed armchair that faced his desk, she crossed her lean, honey-colored legs. "Cream, no sugar, please."

When he handed her the cup, he noted how her lashes framed her warm, brown eyes.

She smiled impishly at him. "How's that M & M supply?"

From the bottom drawer of his desk he took out the glass candy jar. "I'm beginning to suspect you came back for these."

"Uh-oh," she said. "I've been found out. Behind my charitable facade beats the heart of a chocaholic."

Without responding, he studied her. What *had* brought her back? Automatically he glanced at his watch. "Damn. It's eleven o'clock already." He'd better get moving if he wanted to make his lunch date with the mayor. "Grab your coffee and come on."

"Where are we going?" she asked, a note of surprise in her voice.

"To the basketball court out back."

"Why? Can't we talk in here?"

While he held the door open, she threw her purse over one shoulder, then tried to balance her coffee cup, fishing tackle box, and M & M's in her other hand.

"Nope," he said. "Every morning I shoot fifty baskets. Rain, shine, or earthquakes. I didn't think you'd be back, so I made plans to have lunch with the mayor in an hour. Either I exercise now or not until tomorrow. And you wouldn't want to be around me if I hadn't worked out, trust me."

Together they walked down the hall. He knew he probably sounded rude. But he'd learned long ago that the key to self-discipline lay in sticking to a daily routine—and breaking it for nothing but the direst of emergencies.

"You make it sound like shooting baskets is some kind of sacred ritual," she said.

They walked through the door that led to a small courtyard behind the shelter. "In a way, it is."

Stripping off his white shirt and narrow tie, he hung them on a hook on the back wall. Then, kneeling, he changed into his tennis shoes. As usual, Mrs. Hughes had put out a towel and a clean T-shirt for after his workout. While he tied his laces, he felt Wendy's eyes on him. He usually exercised without an audience. For a moment it felt strange to be bare-chested in front of an adult woman, particularly one he was attracted to. Shaking off that feeling, he began to jog in place. The sun beat down on his bare skin, quickly warming him.

Wendy took a seat on the wooden bench alongside the small court. "This has got to be the most unusual interview I've ever had."

"It isn't over yet. I was rather abrupt when you were here before. Don't feel you have to make a hasty . . ." He stopped, remembering how she'd reacted to the word "commitment" the last time they'd talked. "A hasty decision to work here."

"Something tells me you were going to say 'hasty commitment.' " Shielding her eyes from the sun, she asked, "Am I right?"

"You are."

He continued to run in place. Evaluating runaway kids had taught him that waiting was sometimes the best way to elicit information.

After several moments, she shifted uncomfortably on the bench. "I feel like I'm under a microscope. This is the second time you've questioned if I'm serious about teaching. I'm here. I've got my supplies. What else do you need to know?"

As he leaned down to pick up a basketball from the bench next to her, he caught a whiff of her light perfume. "I want to know more about you. Ask you a few questions."

"Fire away."

After dribbling up to the backboard, he made several baskets in rapid succession. "All I know is that you make unusual furniture. Tell me more about yourself."

"Well, I'm nowhere near as good a basketball player as you." She laughed, a sweet, husky sound that reverberated deep inside him. "I think exercising is good—*in principle.* The closest I come to it is a long, slow walk in Golden Gate Park—usually with an ice-cream bar in hand."

Repressing a smile, he said, "Go on."

"I'm twenty-nine. I went to U.C., Santa Cruz, where I got my undergraduate degree in Aesthetic Studies."

Grimacing, he crouched to make a difficult shot. The ball flew in a perfect arc, easily making the mesh basket. "Aesthetic Studies was a real major?"

"Yeah, yeah, I know it sounds a little hokey, but what can I say? It was a hangover from the seventies—when even college bureaucrats got carried away. But the program was really quite good." Shrugging, she smiled good-naturedly. "Let's see. What else do you want to know?"

For a few moments he dribbled the ball back and forth while he studied her. The sunlight picked out red highlights in her hair. She seemed at home in her body—not like the kids at the shelter, who were always fidgeting and wouldn't look anyone in the eye unless they were angry. He found her very sexy. "What did you do with your Aesthetics Studies major?"

"Nothing much." She turned her head to look through the fence that separated his property from the next-door neighbor. "For a year I did illustrations in an architectural firm. But I didn't like it—felt too hemmed in by a nine-to-five job. So I left. Then on a whim, I sold everything I had and traveled around the world."

She turned back to look at him, her curls windblown against her cheek.

With a will of their own, his eyes traced the curve of her shoulders, breasts, and hips. "Traveling alone is a daring thing for a young woman to do."

"Daring or stupid. I was only twenty-three and thought I could handle anything. Luckily, I didn't have any real problems." She let one café-au-lait-colored leg swing back and forth.

How would it feel to run his hands up the smooth skin of her slender calves and then . . . ? Wiping the sweat from his eyes, he forced himself to sound casual as he said, "Sounds like fun."

"It was. I did a couple of volunteer jobs, too. Worked in a soup kitchen in Calcutta, feeding hungry kids. Then in Brazil, I taught farmers ways to help save the rain forests. That sort of thing."

Her heart was in the right place, he thought. His breath coming in quick spurts, he finished another rapid series of baskets. "How'd you end up in the city?"

"Two years ago I visited a friend here, then decided to stay. I started designing my own furniture. I've been lucky enough to be able to support myself. Does that give you an idea of who I am?"

"Yes." He absorbed what she'd said. Like her clothes and furniture, she was different, out of the ordinary. He felt drawn to her independent spirit. But she'd been involved in so many things for such a young woman, would she stick to a project for very long? She seemed to start off with enthusiasm, until something new claimed her attention.

After making his last basket, he took a drink from his plastic water bottle. With the clean towel, he wiped the sweat from his face and chest. Looking over, he caught Wendy's glance. For a long moment, they stared at each other, until she broke the connection. Had she felt the same sensual awareness that drew him to her? He couldn't be sure. Too bad he was such a novice at this.

He pulled on the clean T-shirt, then checked his watch: eleven-fifteen. When this interview was over, he'd have to take a quick shower before he left for lunch. He sat next to her on the wooden bench. "These questions probably seem odd, but I have to look out for my kids."

"I understand." She smiled warmly at him. "I hope you believe I'm trustworthy."

"Everything else in these kids' lives is in chaos. They need to know they can rely on us—no matter what pranks they pull."

"Are they all runaways?"

"Most. Some have been thrown out by their parents." He patted his forehead with the towel, then draped it over his shoulder. "They've usually been on the streets before they end up here. Every once in a while, the court sends us a kid. They can be rude, threatening, even violent. I'm afraid when you find out what you've let yourself in for, you may not want to stay."

"I wasn't expecting the boy and girl next door—"

He continued as if she hadn't interjected anything. "So if you plan to back out, Ms. Valdez, do it now."

"I have no intention of backing out."

Noting the stubborn look that settled on her striking features, he felt another wave of attraction move through his body—and ruthlessly suppressed it. Now was not the time.

"You still don't understand." He gave her the unyielding look that he saved for his most hard-to-handle kids. "No dabblers, no part-time do-gooders, no 'I'm going to save the world' types wanted."

"In other words, no flakes need apply."

"You got it." Leaning back against the chain link fence, he waited to hear how she'd tell him off.

"To set the record straight, I am not a flake. And I'm not afraid of a bunch of teenagers—even kids like these. If I was that timid, I wouldn't have traveled around the world by myself."

She had a point. "Working with angry kids takes a different kind of courage than traveling alone."

"I see exactly what you're doing. You don't think I'm strong enough to work here, so you're trying to drive me away by acting like a drill sergeant." Her voice softened, losing its edge. "And I would've left long ago, but I can tell that you're just protecting these kids that no one else wants."

Jack's eyes met hers. She understood. That made him feel good. Very good.

"I think what you do here is wonderful," she said. In an unexpected gesture, she put her hand on his jean-clad knee.

A shock ran through him at the fleeting contact. He wanted to take her slender fingers in his, feel her softness.

She removed her hand. "The kids are lucky to have you on their side. So don't worry. I won't take the job unless I'm ready to stick to it." She gave a jaunty grin. "Fair enough?"

He momentarily forgot that she expected an answer as he absorbed her breathtaking smile.

Her voice penetrated the haze he was in. "Does that seem fair to you?"

"Fair enough."

"Why don't you give me a tour?" she said, putting her empty coffee cup down on the bench. "Show me how you do things—and then I'll decide if I belong here or not."

"Sure." He'd introduce her to some of the most troubled kids. That would be the true litmus test.

Together they walked down the main hallway to the dining room filled with long tables and utilitarian chairs. "We eat three meals a day, family style. You'd be surprised at how important it is to the kids—as much as they say they hate it at first."

"Is it because this becomes their home?"

"You got it. They want badly to belong somewhere." Leaning against the doorframe, he settled into his familiar spiel. "All of our kids are here because they're in some sort of crisis. We've got every teenage problem imaginable: drugs, violence, pregnancy."

"Being a teenager can be the pits," she said with feeling. "It was hard enough when I was a kid, but I'd hate to be one today."

"The stakes are higher today," he agreed. That was the second time she'd mentioned a painful adolescence. Scanning her face, he wondered what the guarded look in her eyes meant.

He took her to two neighboring rooms filled with rows of beds set up dormitory style. "We have space for thirty kids. With a few exceptions, most only stay here for three months maximum."

"What happens when they leave?"

Barely registering her question, he caught himself staring at her again, wondering what it would feel like to run his hand over the soft-looking skin of her cheek. He wasn't used to having physical attraction cloud his thinking; he'd spent years suppressing just such stirrings.

He blinked. "What did you say?"

She repeated her question with a smile. "What happens when the kids leave here?"

"We reunite families when we can. When we can't, we send the kids to other agencies who provide long-term care."

"Don't any of the kids stay longer?"

"Rarely. Lamar's an exception. He's here on probation, so he'll probably stay for six months."

"Oh, really?" Astonishment registered on her face. "Aside from being a little, uh, flirtatious, he seems like a neat kid. Why's he here?"

"He's worked as a pimp since he was twelve." Would she be shocked? No, she looked sad. "The police finally got tired of pulling him into the station for talks, so they busted him last month."

"Ah! So that's why he tried to pick me up."

He did a double take. "Lamar propositioned you?"

"The second I pulled up to drop off my furniture."

He let out a loud laugh. "You gotta admit the kid's got chutzpah. Everything is a business opportunity to him. He'd be a wonderful entrepreneur if only he'd direct his energies in *legal* channels."

"What's he interested in—besides girls, that is?"

"Graffiti and computer games."

"Graffiti, hmm." She seemed to ponder something. "Some graffiti artists are genuinely talented. Maybe he'd like to learn calligraphy or lettering."

"That's a good idea." Reluctantly he admitted, "I hadn't thought of that." After rounding a corner in the hall, he stopped outside a door with a small window. Inside, another class was under way. "We have three counselors on staff, plus tutors from the San Francisco school district and special classes on applying for jobs."

"What about college preparation?"

"Get real. Few of our kids make it through high school—let alone college. Take Pam, for example." He pointed to a plain girl with short bleached blond hair who slouched in a chair in the corner, resentfully eyeing the other kids. "I'd be happy if she'd get into high school."

"How'd she end up on the street?" she asked softly.

"Her father beat her, so she ran away. She's been arrested for shoplifting and attacking other kids. She got here last week. Under her anger, she's scared and hurt. But she won't let anybody get close enough to help her."

"Sounds like she feels pretty bad about herself."

"You try to survive the street with a bunch of predators circling around you, and you'd feel bad about yourself, too." He couldn't check the contempt he felt for the people who preyed on street kids.

"I never wanted to think about what it would be like to be a young girl on the streets." She shivered. "It's scary."

"That's Gillian," he said brusquely, pointing to a pretty girl with dark blond hair who sat in the middle of the group, flirting with her big blue eyes. "She's fourteen and worked for a year on the streets as a prostitute."

"The poor kid! Doesn't she have a family to go home to?"

"They disowned her. After she leaves here, she'll go to a halfway house—if there's an opening."

"What happens if you can't find a place?"

"She'll probably end up back on the streets." For a moment, a wave of weariness washed over him, then he pushed it away. Despair never got one anywhere. They continued on down the hall.

"Those are just a few of our residents," he said, stopping outside his office. "They need us to accept them—no matter what mistakes they've made. And we can't always save a kid, no matter how hard we try. Can you handle that?"

Wendy looked up into his face, noting the strength stamped there and the warning in his blue eyes. He was still testing her. "Yes. At first, I offered to help on a whim. But the more I see, the more I feel I belong here." As soon as she said that, she realized it was true. These kids reminded her of herself when she was a teenager—only they had bigger problems.

Preceding her into his office, Jack went to sit at his desk.

"You've mentioned your adolescence several times. Didn't you like being a teenager?"

Feeling momentarily vulnerable and exposed, she turned to stare blindly out the window. "It was the worst time of my life."

"What happened?"

"Oh, it sounds melodramatic now, but then it was awful. I didn't fit in anywhere, thought I was ugly, was sure nobody liked me. We're talking major insecurity." She fidgeted in the armchair that faced his desk. "My parents were divorcing, so they didn't have time to figure out why their daughter was falling apart. I disappeared into a shell. Wouldn't talk to anyone—except my teachers and two best friends."

His vivid dark eyes scanned her face. "Sounds painful."

"I'm fine now," she said, consciously straightening up in the chair. "But when I look back, I have to laugh a little. I had no perspective whatsoever."

"Teenage tunnel vision," he said wryly.

"Exactly! In my mind, there was no such thing as life after high school. If Paul Curtin—the football captain—and his crowd didn't like me, I might as well be dead. Looking at these kids, though, I realize I was lucky."

He leaned forward. "It's hard to imagine you as a tormented teen. You're so pretty and self-assured."

"Thank you."

"What changed?"

"I've worked hard on myself." She felt flustered under his probing stare.

Finally he nodded as if satisfied. "It takes courage to face your demons."

"Thanks." That was perceptive of him. Few people recognized that it took conscious effort to untie the straitjacket of one's past. "Seeing the kids here makes some of those old, raw feelings resurface. If I hadn't had my drawing and a couple of great teachers on my side, I could easily have turned to drugs. Or something worse." When she looked in his eyes, she saw the last walls of his resistance crumble.

"So you feel a kinship for these kids."

"I do." An image flashed in her mind of Lamar's cocky grin, Pam's sullen stare, and Gillian's too loud laugh. "It would be great to get a chance to give back some of the support I got when I was a teenager."

"Welcome aboard, Wendy." Coming to stand next to her, he gripped her hand in a firm shake. "I think we're lucky to have you."

Three

After making arrangements to start teaching Thursday, Wendy headed for home. On the way she stopped at the grocery store and picked up some fresh sourdough bread, cold cuts, and sodas for dinner. Opening the door to her apartment-cum-studio, she rubbed the graying head of Elsie, her Doberman pinscher.

"Hey, girl. Keeping the riffraff away?" Elsie growled convincingly, then slobbered on Wendy's hand. Spotting her roommate, Wendy asked, "Still working, Nate?"

"Got to get this done." The blond man with the slight build of a boy on the edge of adolescence knelt in the center of the living room. After plastering glue-soaked paper on a cloth sculpture that resembled an accident between the Golden Gate Bridge and the Transamerica Pyramid, he rocked back on his haunches. He tilted his head and tapped his stubby finger against his chin. "It still needs something. But what? What?"

"Hmmm," she said noncommittally, knowing a rhetorical question when she heard one.

Nathan had been one of her best friends since high school. He'd lived across the street, but had grown up to be anything but the boy next door. They'd lost contact, then run into each other two years before when they were hunting for apartments in the area south of Market Street. Since they'd each wanted enough space to do their artwork, they decided to rent a spacious three-bedroom loft together.

"Argh! That's it for now." Turning eyes the color of opaque green marbles in her direction, Nathan asked, "So what's the story with those cute little delinquents?"

"Be kind." She playfully bopped him on the head with the loaf of sourdough bread. "Those kids have got it rough."

"Honey, don't we all?"

She smiled at him. "You're incorrigible."

"That's why you love me, isn't it?"

"No, I love you out of habit."

He gave her a dirty look, then followed her into the narrow kitchen at the back of the apartment, where sunlight streamed in through two floor-to-ceiling windows.

"Tell me about the shelter," he said, pulling a tall stool up to the butcher block table that also served as telephone message center and art display counter. "Did you meet up with that big lug you told me about last time?"

"The big lug is Jack O'Connor." She started to make two turkey sandwiches, tossing tidbits to Elsie, who enthusiastically caught them in midair.

He frowned. "Do we feed the dog from the table?"

"Absolutely not. Would I do a thing like that?" She lobbed another slice into Elsie's waiting mouth.

He sighed. "Never mind. So what's this guy like?"

"Other than being a control freak, he's okay."

" 'Okay'?" Her friend scooted closer. "Is that all you can say? I want *details!*"

"He's admirable, very disciplined—"

"Yeah, yeah, yeah. Tell your mom. I want to know what he *looks* like."

"He's a great big guy. Good-looking in a dark, brooding, Heathcliff sort of way. He has black hair that's a little curly, a great butt, and the bluest eyes I've ever seen—"

"But you're not interested, right?"

"Not my type." So why had she felt on edge when Jack turned those dark eyes on her? Why had she blushed for the first time in years? Okay, so he was attractive, but that didn't mean she'd ever want to get involved with him. "He's too intense, too driven. I want to live a little, not run myself into an early grave."

"I'm with you there."

"Get this," she said. "He interviewed me outside on a basketball court."

"Why, in God's name?"

Quickly she outlined why Jack hadn't left time in his schedule for her. "So he had to shoot fifty baskets before he had lunch with the mayor."

"You couldn't have kept me inside that place with a pack of pit bulls." Nathan dabbed the corners of his mouth with his napkin. "The man sounds incredibly rude."

"But it wasn't personal. He's just incredibly determined. Determined to look out for the kids. Determined to be in good physical shape. Determined—"

"To be a pain in the neck," he added darkly.

Used to his interruptions, she ignored him. "You know what it is? You see that he's really committed to what he does. So you overlook his brusqueness."

"Hmmm. He's starting to sound intriguing. Sure you're not interested?"

"Positive, Nate. It's kind of hard to cozy up to someone who reminds me of a drill sergeant." So why had she told Jack so much? Although she was relatively open about herself, she wasn't usually *that* open. "I like a man who knows how to enjoy life."

"So do I." He lifted his eyebrows suggestively.

"He's not your type either."

"Too bad." Picking up his plate and silverware, the blond man carried them to the sink. "I better get back to work. Thanks for the grub, *chérie*. Just leave the dishes, and I'll do them later."

On Thursday Wendy showed up at Valencia House thirty minutes early. When she entered his office, Jack looked up from his paperwork. His dark hair curled damply on his broad forehead, as if he'd just showered. An image flashed in her mind of him on the basketball court, the muscles of his bare chest glistening under the hot sun. Why was she thinking of that? The guy didn't appeal to her, right?

They exchanged hellos, then he walked around his desk and perched on its edge.

"Before your first class," he said, "let me give you some pointers. You're not here to win a popularity contest. Don't let the kids get away with things now, thinking it'll get better. It won't. Remember, you can always get softer, but you can't get tougher."

Through the open window she heard the yelps and screams of kids playing basketball. "I'm not going to have a lot of discipline problems, am I?"

"Not if you start off right. The school rules are: no street clothes, no talking back, no profanity, and no late work."

"Sounds like boot camp."

"Trust me. These kids need discipline as much as they need love." From the back pocket of his form-fitting black jeans, he pulled two keys. "The front and back door are always locked—with buzzers for security. Interior doors stay unlocked. We work on an honor system here."

Her cold fingers met his warm hand. As she quickly dropped the keys into her purse, she remembered the computers bolted to the desks. "Honor system? What about the Apple computers?"

"Too much temptation will undermine anybody. We're optimists, not fools." From the squeaky middle drawer of his desk, he took out a battered flashlight. "Keep this in case the electricity goes out—which happens too often. It usually takes about thirty minutes to get it going again."

She was beginning to feel as if she were in a war zone. "What do I do if a kid acts up?"

"Send him to me. Immediately. I don't tolerate misbehavior. We have too many street kids who want to stay here to put up with some fool who wants to ruin a class for the other students."

He sounded awfully harsh, but she wouldn't waste time arguing. Once she was in her classroom, she'd do what she thought was best. Playing things by ear usually worked for her.

"I need to set up my stuff. Can you show me my classroom?"

"This way." He led her down the main hall to a small classroom with desks that looked as though they'd been there since World War II. They'd have to go. Much too depressing.

"Make yourself comfortable," he said, as he turned to leave. "The kids will be here soon."

A wave of panic rose in her throat at the thought of facing ten or fifteen hostile teenagers who probably had as much interest in art as the attendant who worked at the corner gas station. "Wait! Isn't there anything else I need to know?"

"Relax, you'll do fine."

"And if I don't . . . ?"

"Just holler. See that door over there?" He pointed to a darkened entry at the back of the room, obscured by shadows. "It leads to a hall that connects with the back door of my office. I'll leave the door open so I can look in without the kids knowing I'm there. It's my policy to observe each teacher's first class."

"That makes me feel better."

"We'll talk later."

"Thanks." If she survived this first class.

Going over to her desk, he lined it up precisely with the chalkboard. "The room's been empty for a while." He wiped his dusty hands on his dark jeans. "Sorry we didn't get a chance to clean it up. Feel free to rearrange things if you want."

"Thanks. I will." He had no idea what he'd just given her permission to do. Valencia House was orderly, but too much like a state penitentiary for her taste. If she could redo it, she'd start by trashing most of the old furniture and then repainting the classrooms in something besides institutional green. Maybe neon yellow or sweet potato orange. She began to feel excited again. This might be fun after all.

"Good luck," he said, then walked out, leaving the back door a few inches ajar behind him.

Eyes sparkling, Mrs. Hughes put the last piece of slightly singed pineapple upside-down cake on Jack's desk. "Under those rather colorful clothes I just *knew* Miss Valdez had a good heart."

"She'll need more than a good heart to survive here." He took a big bite of cake, then a drink of freshly brewed coffee. "Our kids can drive the calmest person crazy."

"They are rascals, aren't they?"

He shook his head fondly at his assistant. Not many people would characterize the often disrespectful and sometimes violent teenagers as "rascals." When the pressures of work began to make him pessimistic, Mrs. Hughes would say something that reminded him that what he needed was *more* faith—not less. "I think Ms. Valdez thinks I'm too strict with our 'rascals.' "

"A lot of people make that mistake before they get to know you well," she said indignantly. "Those young people are lucky to have you on their side. Wendy's a smart girl. It won't take her long to realize what a good man you are."

To his surprise, he liked the way that sounded. What did it take to qualify as a good man in Wendy's book, he wondered.

"I couldn't run this shelter without your help, Thelma." He lifted his coffee cup in a salute to the older woman. "Sometimes I think the only thing that keeps Lamar here is your homemade chocolate chip cookies."

Mrs. Hughes pooh-poohed his comments, then bustled out of the room.

Alone in his office, Jack thought about his attraction to Wendy and the problems it presented. Ever since he was a young boy, he'd been driven by one overriding goal—the burning desire to become a priest. Everything else—friends, sports, his first sexual stirrings—had been pushed aside so that he could prepare for his future calling.

Until he'd dropped out of seminary school two years ago.

Until his doubts about his commitment to his future profession had become greater than his faith.

Wendy was the first woman to genuinely catch his interest since he'd gained his newfound freedom. So what did he do now? This was unknown terrain to him. Turning his swivel chair, he watched the breeze rustle the leaves of a large eucalyptus tree outside his window. The day was crisp, the sky blue and cloudless. The sort of day that made you feel anything could happen.

Leaning forward, he began to drum his fingers on his desk. A smile made itself at home on his face—the kind of smile that put his students on guard. He didn't know what he'd do next, but this was going to be one hell of a ride.

At one P.M. no one had arrived in Wendy's classroom. At five after one, she still sat at the large, scarred desk at the front of the room, tracing the name "Allison" that someone had carved in the wood long ago. As the minutes ticked by, her annoyance grew. She had plenty of her own work to do instead of sitting here killing time.

At ten after one, the door opened and in sauntered Lamar, Gillian, and Pam. She waited expectantly for other kids to arrive, but no one materialized. Was this her class?

"Sorry we're dragging tail, teach," Lamar said. "Our group therapy session got a little hairy, and they made us stay late. Wouldn't you know, someone was blabbing on about committing suicide again."

Wendy tried not to let shock register on her features. The things these kids had to deal with on a daily basis were mind-boggling. "I'm sorry to hear that."

"Happens at least once a week. Sometimes I wish one of them would do it, just so we didn't have to *hear* about it again." He shot a look at Pam, who stared straight ahead, refusing to make eye contact.

Although Wendy realized Lamar was dominating the room, she had no idea what to do about it. Sheer terror gripped her as she imagined losing control of the class before it had officially started. "Let's get started on our first art project. . . ."

"I hope you don't expect us to make any of that ugly furniture you brought." Lamar gave her a challenging look.

Gillian smothered a giggle. "Don't be mean, Lamar."

Pam loudly scraped her black cowboy boots on the floor, then slouched lower in her seat. "Give her hell, Lamar."

"I'm serious, girl." He adjusted his black hairnet—an accessory Wendy had seen other inner-city kids wear—then sprawled back in his chair. "If she wanted to donate something, what's the matter with VCRs or hi-resolution TVs?" He snorted in disgust. "Hell, she probably gives clothes for Christmas."

So Jack hadn't been kidding. Her students were ready to take her on a ride if she didn't grab the reins, and fast.

"Lamar," Wendy said in an even tone. "Come on up here."

"What for?"

"I saw your handwriting, and I want you to draw some letters on the board for me."

"I'm good, it's true." After bowing to the two girls, he strutted up to the chalkboard on the wall. "What do you want me to write?"

What would cut through his defenses? Handing him a piece of hot pink chalk, she improvised, "Your full name and your father's full name."

"How'd you know I had a beautiful name, teach?" He wrote in large and very distinctive handwriting on the board, intoning as he went along, "Lamar David Washington. Sounds like a Supreme Court justice, don't it?"

Under her breath, Pam said, "Or a pimp."

Sensing an imminent explosion, Wendy said, "Gillian, you write your name here. On the wall."

"Won't I get into trouble?"

"No," Wendy said with a conviction she didn't completely feel. "It's my classroom, and I'm giving you permission."

Although she tried to stop herself, her eyes moved to the door at the back of the room. No sign of Jack. Good. She'd rather explain this to him after the fact. Turning to Pam, she said, "Come up here by my desk and draw a design on the hardwood floor."

Without changing her glum expression, Pam took the chalk.

"Hey," Lamar said. "Why didn't you ask *me* to write on the wall or the floor?"

"I never give the best jobs to someone who insults my 'ugly' furniture. Keep that in mind for next time."

He grinned briefly before he grumbled. "Okay, okay, but you never said we'd be writing on the wall."

When the students were done, she had them look at one another's handiwork, then discuss what they'd done.

"Look at Lamar's elegant script," she said enthusiastically. "See how the chalk works on the surface it was intended for." With her thumb, she deliberately smeared a corner of a hot pink letter written on the chalkboard.

"Hey, hey, hey! Careful with my masterpiece."

Walking over to Gillian's work, she smiled at the childish writing style. "Notice how dramatic the pink chalk looks on the green wall."

"Looks like dried Pepto-Bismol to me," Lamar said dismissively.

"That's a wonderful description!" Wendy laughed.

The boy's scowl turned into a cocky smile. Then they scrutinized Pam's boxy handwriting done on the floor planks.

"It looks like it was hard to write on," Gillian offered in a friendly voice.

"Masterful deduction," Pam sneered. "Ever think about becoming a brain surgeon?"

Seeing Gillian's wounded expression, Lamar glared at Pam.

"Every surface reacts differently," Wendy said quickly. "Sometimes you want the obvious match, like chalk on chalkboard." Dipping a sponge in bright orange paint, she took it over to the wall. "But sometimes you need to experiment a bit to find something more exciting." She dabbed the orange paint onto the pink chalk. The two colors ran together.

"How fresh!" Gillian exclaimed. "It looks like a sunset over Golden Gate Bridge."

Animated talk and laughter filled the room as the students tried chalk and paint on different types of paper, the wall, and the floor. Wendy smiled to herself, knowing she'd snagged their interest.

Jack hung up the phone, then jogged down the hall. Convincing an employer to take a chance on one of his kids had required longer than he'd expected. Wendy's class had been going on for almost thirty minutes. He didn't like to wait that long before he checked in on a new teacher.

As he got near her classroom, he heard raucous laughter. He almost tripped. Laughter on the first day usually meant trouble. Big trouble. He hoped they weren't tormenting her too badly. Stepping inside, he sat down unobtrusively on a chair in the corner. The students' backs were to him while Wendy sat hunched over in the middle of the floor. Adrenaline surged through his body. If they'd done anything to hurt her . . .

Before he could follow that thought any further, she rocked back on her knees. He saw that she'd been leaning over a large piece of butcher paper covered with bright paint. She'd kicked off her shoes, her lovely face glowed with happiness, and something pink dusted one side of her dark curls. She was even prettier than he'd first thought.

"Your turn, Lamar." Wendy's voice sounded carefree.

Jack watched in bewilderment as Lamar put on a blindfold, took a paintbrush, then made designs on the paper. What in the world was going on?

"Teach, this is hard," Lamar moaned, then chuckled. "Can't I look for just a sec? Puleeeeeze?"

Wendy laughed, a low, husky sound that sent a ripple of awareness through Jack. "Okay, you can look now."

Lamar pulled off his blindfold. "All right!"

Amusement, then relief, swept over Jack; Wendy had the class eating out of her hand. He cared about every staff member's safety, but with her he felt a surge of protectiveness that took him aback with its force.

Looking around, he spotted the pink handwriting on the wall, the desk, and the floor. He shook his head, exasperation edging out the feeling of relief. She was doing better than he'd expected, but he couldn't let her ruin school property. They'd have to have a little talk about her teaching methods.

Outside the shelter, Jack hopped in his car and went to visit his old mentor, Father Daniel Quinn. For years the priest had been a father figure. Reaching St. Evangeline's Church, Jack rapped on the intricately engraved door at the back of the rectory. After a few moments, the heavy door creaked open, scraping to a halt on the uneven stone floor.

Father Quinn peered out, his lined, genial face creasing into a smile at the sight of his former student. Although in his seventies, the priest had a youthful air. Gesturing for Jack to come in, Father Quinn said, "Jack, my boy! What a pleasure. You're looking well."

"Thank you, Father." Jack stepped into the cool, dark corridor. "You got a minute?"

"I was just on my way out to the garden for a cup of tea and some butter cookies. Care to join me?" The priest smoothed down his black clothes and gave a puckish smile.

He shared Jack's childlike delight in sweets. A sudden image of Wendy with a handful of M & M's flashed in Jack's mind. He couldn't seem to get her out of his thoughts. "Sounds good."

"It'll be like old times." The older man's bushy gray eyebrows rose in obvious delight.

Together Jack and the portly priest headed down the corridor that opened onto a pathway sprinkled with leaves. There they walked under a canopy of sycamore trees that led to a glen.

Jack enjoyed the sloping trail as he had so many times in the past. The Church of St. Evangeline had been built a hundred years ago on a large estate donated by a repentant gold miner on his deathbed. The city of San Francisco had grown up around it, and now the church occupied a prime piece of real estate near the Presidio.

When they reached the glen, Father Quinn settled himself in one of the gray wrought-iron chairs that sat around a café table. Jack sat across from him. Sunlight fell on the carpet of broken leaves at their feet.

The older man poured them each a cup of tea, then passed a

plate piled high with fresh butter cookies. "So what brings you here today? One of the kids?"

"No, me this time." Leaning back in the chair, Jack let go of the energy that drove him through life, letting himself hear the background sounds of nature: birds chirping, a lizard rustling under a bush, and wind in the trees. "I've met a woman I like."

The priest pulled out a cherrywood pipe and packed it with sweet-smelling tobacco in quick, expert movements. "Once you quit seminary school, I knew it wouldn't be long before someone caught your eye."

Up until two years before, Jack had trained under the elderly priest's guidance. While Jack had admired Father Quinn's selflessness and dedication to his calling, it became harder and harder to imagine himself living the life of a priest. Every day he'd watched his mentor tirelessly teach students and counsel parishioners, then, late at night, go home alone to a sparsely decorated one-room apartment, his books, and a mangy gray cat.

Finally Jack couldn't kid himself any longer. He had admitted that he wanted a wife, a family, and a home much more than he wanted to become a priest. Although he'd expected Father Quinn to try to talk him out of his decision, the older man had listened without judging. Jack now counted him as one of his best friends.

Leveling his bright gaze at Jack, the priest said, "Tell me about her."

"Very pretty, but that's not what attracts me. She's got a real soft side, even though she tries to hide it. Independent, wants to do things her way." Jack looked off into the distance. "There's something between us, some kind of spark, but I don't know what exactly. Doesn't stop me dreaming, though—from feeling like a fish out of water."

"To be expected." The older man took a puff on his pipe and held the smoke in for a moment. "You spent years repressing your sexual feelings. And now you have to deal with them."

"I'm like an awkward teenager." Grinning self-deprecatingly, Jack added, "A teenager in a thirty-year-old's body—and an *inexperienced* thirty-year-old at that."

"So you're not certain what to do next."

"Right. Once I decided I wasn't cut out to be a priest, I assumed everything else would be easy. I never really thought about what I'd do once I met someone."

"Jack, things that are hard for other people have always come easily for you. Perhaps too easily. But this is something you don't know much about. Not yet, at least."

"I don't want to fall on my face."

The priest lit another match and held the yellow flame against the bowl of the pipe until it caught and turned the tobacco red. "What would you tell one of your teenagers if he came to you with this sort of problem?"

Jack stopped drumming his fingers on the small table. Leave it to Father Quinn to see the obvious and make it clear. "Take his time, get to know the girl, and let the trust between them develop."

"That's good advice." The priest poured another cup of fragrant tea from the generously curved pot. "Time is a better friend than most of us realize."

Four

On Tuesday, Jack watched Wendy walk jauntily toward him, still glowing from her experience with her first class. A twinge of guilt assailed him when he thought about the conversation that lay ahead, but he thrust that feeling aside. He had a right to be annoyed. After all, she'd virtually let her students deface school property.

"Oh, Jack, the class went so well!" Sinking into the armchair in front of his desk, she let out a sigh of contentment. "I think I'm really going to like teaching here."

"I'm glad you had a good time."

She smiled at him, an open, uncomplicated smile that almost compelled him to grin back.

Steeling himself, he continued, "But there are a few things we have to talk about." His voice sounded harsher than he'd intended, and he tried to soften it. "I was concerned with what I saw when I sat in on your class—"

"Hold on a sec," she said, lifting her hand to stop him. "Let me guess. You probably didn't like the paint on the wall, did you?"

"Or on the chalkboard or the floor," he added wryly.

"I'm sure it looked bad, but let me explain."

"Go right ahead." It wasn't fair that she was so appealing. Clearly he'd have to work to remain objective about her. Now that he wasn't denying his feelings of attraction, life had become much more complex.

She rose and began to pace the room. Emotions flitted across her expressive face as she spoke. "When the students first came in, I was terrified. We're talking Panic City." Clutching the soft wool of her sweater above her heart, she widened her brown eyes, an exaggerated look of fear on her face. "You know what I mean?"

Perhaps she'd missed her calling; she'd have made a good actress. In melodramas. "I know what you mean. They can be an intimidating bunch."

"When Lamar started to take over the class, I had to find some way to grab control. I mean, it's not as if I *planned* to paint on the wall. The idea just came into my head." She plopped back in her chair and smiled, two dimples appearing in her cheeks. "And it worked, you gotta admit."

"This time." He strode to the window. Outside, he could see the girls' basketball team performing a drill. They looked orderly, in sync and disciplined. Before one could have freedom, rules had to be clearly established. There was no room for chaos at Valencia House—even if someone as delightful as Wendy innocently introduced it. "Just because it worked this time doesn't mean it will keep working."

"Oh, come on! Paint can be washed off."

"That's not the point. We don't want the kids to think it's okay to deface school property."

"Don't you think that's a tad unfair?" she asked with a chuckle. "I was *hardly* doing that. As a matter of fact, I had Lamar stay after and wash off the paint. Nothing was damaged."

A part of him wanted to give in to her personal brand of logic. There was a captivating quality to her as she sat there, utterly relaxed and free-spirited. But if he gave in, no one would benefit. Not Wendy. Not the students.

"I've worked too long with these kids to be fooled by a passing enthusiasm on their part. They can change as fast as the weather—and be almost as dangerous. Granted, no real damage was done—to the room. But what about your credibility as teacher?"

"What, teachers can't be fun?" A look of doubt crossed her features—and it disturbed him.

But he knew he had to warn her. "These kids will think you're a big pushover if you let them paint all over the place. Believe me. I've seen this sort of thing happen before."

"Jeez, I feel like you're giving me a sermon." Her smile took the sting from her words. "Did you ever consider becoming a preacher?"

Scanning her face, he swallowed. No, there was no way she could know about his background. It was just an uncanny comparison. "Sorry," he said hoarsely. "I have a tendency to become passionate about the things I believe in."

"Don't apologize. Just remember there's room for other points of view."

"Okay."

"My methods *are* unorthodox, I'll admit it. But the important thing is that the kids got involved. You saw the class, you saw how much fun they were having. That counts for something."

"Of course, but they need limits. Today they painted on the wall, tomorrow maybe it's the ceiling, then my office. Where's it going to stop?"

"You have to have a little faith." Her tone held a gentle reproach. "In them *and* in me. I can control them. I know it." She searched his face as if she wanted to find a means to convince him, then continued in a soft voice. "How about a deal? You give me a month to try out my methods. If they don't work, I'll use your approach. And if you're right, you get to say 'I told you so' as many times as you want."

He considered her suggestion. Although he was afraid she'd end up hurt and disillusioned, maybe he was wrong. A month wasn't that long; if her plan didn't work out, it wouldn't be a disaster.

She put out her hand in a conciliatory gesture. "What do you say?"

"All right." He took her slender fingers in his. "I'll give you a month. But if there's any damage, you'll be responsible."

"There won't be any damage."

"And if I see that you—or the kids—are in danger of being hurt, I'll call a halt to the whole thing."

"I can take care of myself. And them." She smiled a slow, heart-stopping smile. "Just watch. This will be great. You won't be disappointed."

When school was over on Wednesday, a solitary figure appeared in the hall outside Wendy's classroom. The teenager carefully checked the dark passageway before slipping in through the unlocked door. After waiting to become accustomed to the low level of light in the room, the youth methodically ripped up stacks of paper, tipped over cans of paint, and snapped every paintbrush into tiny pieces. When the room was in shambles, the teenager slipped back outside and disappeared down the hallway on silent feet.

That evening, before Jack returned to his studio apartment near the shelter, he made his customary rounds of the building. When he opened the door to Wendy's classroom, he immediately spotted the destruction.

Stepping inside, he surveyed the scene. Cans of paint littered the floor. Bright rivers of color spilled across the wooden desks, dripped down the blackboard, and puddled on the hardwood floor. The once neat stacks of construction paper had been ripped apart and scattered about the room. Several desks were upended and huge gouges ran across the blackboard.

He clenched his hands into tight balls, refusing to slam his fists into the wall. The waste and senseless violence in the room gave him a sick feeling in his gut. In the year and a half since he'd started the shelter, Valencia House had been defaced with graffiti and pelted with hubcaps, eggs, and even burritos. But he'd never seen anything quite like this disturbing blast of anger within the building. And as much as he didn't want to admit it, chances were good this had been done by one of his kids.

Although he wasn't a parent—yet—he felt as protective of the shelter as if it were a beloved child. So much frustration was expressed in this act; it put him on alert that he had an explosive person in the group of teens. Sometimes when he thought he'd seen everything, the shock of a kid's behavior got through his armor.

He turned at a noise behind him in the hall. Gillian stood at the door, looking scared and very young.

"Wow!" she said in a subdued voice. "This is awful. Who did it?"

"Good question, kiddo. Did you hear or see anything out of the ordinary?"

"No." After glancing around as if the perpetrator might still be in the room, she turned fearful eyes on him. "I didn't see nothing."

Putting his arm around the girl's slight shoulders, he hugged her. He didn't want her to be frightened the way she'd been when she first came off the streets—always waiting for the next attack. "Tomorrow we'll have to do a little detective work, won't we?"

When Gillian realized she wasn't going to be blamed, the tension left her frame. "Yeah. I guess so."

"But first, it sounds like you need a glass of O'Connor's special restorative hot cocoa and a good book to read."

"Yuk, reading!" She made a face, but followed him willingly to the kitchen.

After Jack had fixed a cup of cocoa and given Gillian a well-worn copy of *Catcher in the Rye,* he turned her over to Mrs. Watson, the capable matron who was on duty in the girls' dormitory at night.

Returning to his office, he tried to phone Wendy to tell her about the vandalism. Her line was busy. After several more tries, he slammed down the phone. A restless energy coursed through him. Although he knew it made no logical sense, he had to talk to her *tonight.*

He grimaced at his self-deception.

"You don't need to see her, old boy," he spoke aloud. "You *want* to." He looked at his watch again. Nine-fifteen. If he remembered correctly, she'd said she was a night owl.

Without letting his mind come up with any more reasons for not going, he jotted down her address and took off into the night.

When the doorbell rang, Wendy picked up her baseball bat and cautiously approached her front door. It was either one of Nathan's friends or some undesirable sort who'd wandered upstairs from the street. Normally Elsie, her Doberman, would have beat her to the door, but the dog was at the vet's tonight for minor surgery. After giving a couple of practice swings, Wendy peered through the peephole in the door. What she saw was the last thing she'd expected: the stark, handsome face of Jack O'Connor.

She almost dropped the bat on her foot. What was he doing here at this time of the night?

"It's Jack, Wendy." His deep voice came through the door. "May I come in?"

"Sure. Just a sec." Holding the bat in one hand, she rushed to unlock the seven dead bolts on the door. Thinking of her bare feet, her paint-splattered jeans, and her sweatshirt with holes, she groaned. Any suspicions Jack had about her being a flake would be confirmed when he saw her outfit; she looked like a cartoon of a beatnik.

Finally undoing the last lock, she swung the door wide. "Come in, please."

When he stepped through the doorway, his large frame dwarfed her entry hall. She noticed again how striking he looked with his midnight black hair, his dark clothes, and his blue, blue eyes.

Jack's expression was unreadable as he registered her clothes, the pieces of furniture she'd been painting, and the baseball bat she carried. "Tell me," he said dryly, "are you making furniture or destroying it?"

Nonplussed, she followed the direction of his gaze to her bat, then laughed. "No, no. This is my protection when Elsie, my Doberman, isn't here. She's at the vet's tonight."

"Nothing serious, I hope."

"Nope, just minor surgery. She'll be home tomorrow."

There was an awkward silence. When she looked into the depths of his eyes, excitement slithered down her spine. There was something hidden, almost ominous, about him. She couldn't shake the feeling that he had some dark secret lurking just beneath the surface. Just when she thought she had him figured out, he did something unpredictable. Take tonight, for example. What was he doing here?

"I'm surprised to see you," she said. "Is everything okay?"

"May I?" He lowered his large frame onto her leather couch. Stretching his arm along the back of the sofa, he turned his intense gaze on her. "We've had a problem at the shelter. I tried to call, but your line was busy. Someone vandalized your classroom."

"Oh, my God!" She began to bite the inside of her lower lip. "What happened? Did someone break in?"

"I doubt it. There's no sign of forced entry to the building. I have to assume it was done by one of the kids."

"Really?"

"Yes. Maybe even someone from your class."

She didn't like the way that sounded. "Why do you think that?"

"Because no other room was touched."

Fear tickled her mind. "But what would anyone have against me or my classroom?"

"Don't take it personally. I don't know why they chose your room. It could mean nothing—just bad luck."

"It's weird, though, that right after I start teaching . . . this happens." She felt herself shivering. "What exactly did they do?"

He briefly described the state of her classroom. She began to pace in front of the sofa, mentally reviewing her three students. Then, shaking her head, she said, "I know I've only taught at the shelter for a few days, but I can't believe that any of the kids I met could do that sort of thing."

"There isn't any other likely explanation."

"This is creepy, really creepy." She sank down on the couch next to him. "What should we do?"

"When I clean your classroom tomorrow, I'll look for clues that could tell us who did it."

"I'll help. What time are you going to start?"

"Probably at nine. But that's not necessary."

"No, I want to," she said, smiling at his automatic refusal. He was a man used to doing everything by himself. "It's my class."

His gaze moved from her eyes down to her lips. She felt flustered by his scrutiny. When was the last time she'd felt so aware of every word she said or every breath she took? It was difficult to tell if Jack shared her heightened sensitivity, because he kept his face blank and unreadable.

Still, something made her think he was just as aware of the electrical charge in the room as she was. Even the most innocuous of statements seemed to hang in the air like exhaled breath on a cold day. Visible, bodiless, yet almost tangible.

The buzzing of the doorbell interrupted the tense moment. When she went to answer the door, Jack followed, staying near her in a protective fashion that she found oddly endearing. Nathan tended to regard her as utterly competent; until just this moment, she'd never realized that a part of her longed to feel taken care of in small ways like this.

Through the peephole she spotted a man in a green and white outfit from Verdi's, one of San Francisco's best pizza parlors. She opened the door.

"Large pepperoni with mushrooms and green peppers for the lovely lady." The delivery man winked at her. "This is my last delivery of the night. Gonna need any help finishing this off?"

Wendy sighed. She would hardly have thought her spattered pants and ratty shirt romantic, but apparently this man did. Men often looked at her diminutive size and thought she was an easy target for their come-ons.

Before she could tell the delivery man that he'd just lost his tip, Jack stepped into the man's line of vision. "I don't think we'll need any help, pal, but thanks for the offer."

The man blanched. "No problem, sir. Guess I'm getting a little punchy. End of the night, you know."

She noted with interest that Jack effortlessly commanded respect. It wasn't simply his imposing height and size; it was the way he carried himself—as if he feared nothing.

When the delivery man held out the bill, Jack handed him a twenty, then took the change.

After closing the door, Wendy tried to repay Jack, but he waved her money away. "It's the least I can do when I drop by at this time of night." Taking an appreciative breath, he added, "Besides, the pizza smells great."

"Ah, an ulterior motive!"

"Always."

She shot him a glance, noting the glint in his eyes. He wasn't as innocent or straightforward as she'd first suspected.

"Say no more," she said. She moved the paint cans and brushes from the coffee table to one of her work shelves. "Anyone who can cut an obnoxious delivery man down to size has my undying devotion—and all the pepperoni pizza he can eat."

She went to get plates, beers, and napkins. When she returned, she pulled a large, comfortable pillow next to the coffee table and sat down. "I'm starved."

"Me, too," he said, taking the plate she handed him with a steaming slice of pizza on it. "Do you always eat so late?"

"Only when I'm working—which is almost every night. I've got a couple of orders to fill."

He took a big, cheesy bite out of his slice. "Now, that's what I call good pizza."

"Verdi's is my favorite."

Reaching for his beer, he took a swig. "Is that some of your work over there?"

Next to the wall stood four partially painted chairs of different sizes. Her client had asked for "something wild." Tonight Wendy had tried a few new color and design combinations: leopard spots, pink triangles, and gray UFOs. The effect was dramatic—and pleasing to her eyes.

"Yep," she said "I'm designing some chairs for a client who lives in the Booker Mansion. She owns a safari company in Kenya."

"Safari company." His tone bordered on the sardonic. "I get it. Hence the leopard spots."

"Right."

"And the UFOs?" He lifted one eyebrow.

"Whimsy." Seeing the look of incomprehension on his face, she added, "You always need a little whimsy in your designs."

"I'll take your word for it."

"You don't sound convinced."

"I can't quite see one of those great old mansions decorated in a modern style."

"Okay, okay, out with it." She paused, then forged ahead. "I've been getting vibes from you all along that you don't like my furniture. So why don't you just fess up?"

"I haven't been overly enthusiastic, have I?"

"Nope, you haven't." To her surprise, she felt piqued; she hadn't thought she cared about his opinion of her art. But suddenly it mattered—just a little—whether or not he liked her stuff. She'd have to file that reaction away for examination later.

"You obviously put a lot of effort into your work—and I admire that," he said, speaking carefully as if he were trying to spare her feelings. "But I'm a traditionalist at heart, and I can't say I 'understand' your furniture."

"That's refreshingly honest." She could deal with someone who didn't "understand" her work. Heck, sometimes she didn't understand it herself; she was compelled to do it by some part of herself that was beyond rational thought.

"I'm glad you're not offended," he said.

"No, I'm not." Leaning back on her elbows, she stretched her legs out and crossed her feet at the ankles. "At least you've got the guts to say what you feel. Which is exactly what I'm trying to do with my artwork—so you see, we actually have a lot in common."

"Do we?" he asked, regarding her quizzically.

"I think we do."

She detected a certain softening in his expression, an awareness behind the curtain of reserve. A small smile started on his face and turned into a provocative grin.

An answering smile moved across her face. She had to look away to break the moment of complicity that hovered between them.

My God, did the man have any idea how sexy he was?

She needed to get a grip on herself. Perhaps Nathan was right; maybe it *had* been too long since she'd had a boyfriend. It wasn't like her to be so susceptible to the company of a tall, dark man— however mysterious and attractive. And that was the funny thing, he *was* attractive. She found it hard to believe that at first she'd thought him too severe-looking.

It was up to her to steer the conversation back to safer channels. Now, what had they been talking about? Things in common, that's right. "I'll grant you we're different," she said, "but not as much as I thought originally."

He looked skeptically around her studio. "Well, we don't seem to have the same taste in art or interior decorating."

"Actually, sometimes I like traditional things, too. You should see my bedroom: all white lace, plump pillows, and pastel paintings . . . that sort of thing . . ." Even as she spoke, she cursed herself. "Oh, wait. That sounds like I'm inviting you into my bedroom, which I'm not. Oh, this is coming out sideways. . . ."

She watched a red flush move across his strong cheekbones. Why did she blurt things out without thinking? And why were they both reacting like kids at the mention of her bedroom?

She took a hasty bite out of the pizza to hide her uneasiness. Rolling over, she stretched out on her stomach. When in doubt, look unconcerned. "Good pizza, isn't it?"

"Very good."

Jack deliberately kept his expression neutral. What else could he say? Wendy was obviously embarrassed. So was he. Her comment about seeing her bedroom had caught him off guard. Although he guessed she hadn't meant her words to be a come-on, he couldn't stop his willful mind from painting a picture of Wendy lying naked on her white bed, her cloud of red-brown hair spread across the pillows. Stop, he told himself. Relax. He forced himself to lean back against the couch and simply enjoy the sensation of being with an attractive woman.

The lights in the studio were bright, capturing the highlights in her curly hair. When she took another bite out of her pizza, her tongue darted out to catch a strand of cheese. Intercepting his smile, she rolled her eyes.

"Messy, but fun," she said.

"You're fun to be with." The words slipped out of his mouth before he could stop them.

She raised her eyebrows in surprise, then smiled. "Thanks. You are, too. You know, I didn't think so at first."

"Why not?"

"Because you seemed so stern the first time I met you."

"That's interesting."

Wendy regarded Jack silently for a moment, noticing how he'd relaxed. His dark hair was a little rumpled and he'd lost his military bearing. Leaning back against the couch, he'd stretched his long, muscular legs out before him. His eyes, however, still held an unreadable glint.

"I guess you have to be strict with the kids," she said. "But I got the impression that you always kept yourself in complete control. It's nice to see you loosen up a bit."

"Control *is* very important to me. I've always been a disciplined person." Shrugging, he looked away as if what he was about to say was difficult. "It's only recently that I've realized how much I've missed. I haven't spent many relaxed evenings like this." His dark blue eyes found her face and lingered there. "And I like it."

She felt a little thrill. "I hope I'm not being rude, but somehow I see you as the type of guy who'd be married and have your regulation two point five kids already." She hoped he would tell her she was wrong.

He started, then laughed a low, deep laugh that sent a jolt of excitement up her spine. "No, I've got my eighteen Valencia kids, but that's it. I'm not married—yet."

She savored the word "yet," turning it over in her mind as if it were a piece of sand that had the potential to become a pearl. A moment of silence grew between them—not a companionable silence, but a heavy, intoxicating stillness.

When she looked up, he was staring at her. To her surprise, the next thing she knew, he had stretched out on the rug beside her. Lying on his side, he rested his handsome head on one hand and regarded her.

Because he was such a big man, she couldn't help feeling like a shrimp next to him. That was one reason she normally preferred men nearer her height; she didn't like the discrepancy of physical power. But Jack made her feel both protected and deliciously in danger of being engulfed. She liked the mixed sensation.

"It's comfortable here on the rug." He took another swig of his beer.

"I like it." From this close, she could see the texture of his skin and the healthy sheen of his hair. A darker ring of blue fringed his vivid irises, making his eyes look like agates, with depth inside of depth.

He was examining her, too. She wished she could read the emotions that lay behind his piercing gaze. His controlled quality made him seem unapproachable. Yet his full, sensual-looking mouth made her think he would welcome her touch, that he wanted her kiss as much as she wanted his. She found herself wishing she could piece together the puzzle of who he was.

When he reached out to take her hand, she didn't resist. Slowly he ran his strong, rough fingers over her palm, then traced the shape of her fingers and paint-stained nails. His caress was firm, gentle, erotic.

"Painting is hard on your hands," she said self-consciously. When she tried to pull her hand away, he stopped her.

The warm pressure of his fingers on hers increased. "You have beautiful hands. Soft, warm, and feminine . . ." Lifting his eyes from her hand, he studied her face, lingering on her eyes, then her lips. "You're a very beautiful woman." He spoke as if he were thinking out loud.

Flippant words of denial died on her lips. When he leaned over her, she froze. Not out of fear or indecision, but with anticipation. His warm lips brushed against hers with teasing softness. His eyes questioned her.

"It's okay," she whispered.

He needed on further encouragement. Pulling her against his broad chest, he claimed her with his mouth. His tongue slipped between her lips, deepening the kiss. He tasted good. His mouth explored hers with a hunger that set her blood buzzing through her veins. His kiss was perfect—not sloppy or pushy, but sensual and firm and just right.

For such a large man, he held her with amazing tenderness; she decided she liked how much bigger he was. Rubbing her hands over his chest, she loved the feel of his muscles moving under the thin fabric of his black T-shirt.

He slipped one of his jeans-clad legs between hers. My, the man was a fast mover. A melting sensation flooded her lower belly.

He was masterful and tender at the same time. A dangerous combination. He moved his leg back and forth with agonizing slowness—as if determined to make her crazy with desire. As his strong hands caressed her back, a part of her wanted him to slip his fingers beneath her shirt and touch her naked skin. Another part of her was happy that she didn't have to fend him off. She admitted to herself that women were paradoxical creatures. If he'd made more moves, she would have been angry. But since he wasn't groping her, she wondered why.

Her thoughts were interrupted by the gentle pressure of his lips. His tongue licked inside her mouth in quick, hot movements.

In the midst of their kiss, she heard the sound of a key in the front door. Regretfully she pulled herself away from the warm strength of his hold and tried to get control of her breathing.

She looked at Jack. Rapidly straightening his shirt, he looked a little shell-shocked. Sitting up, she adjusted her sweatshirt and tried to pat her hair into some semblance of order. "That must be Nathan, my roommate."

"Nathan?" His voice sounded gruff.

When she saw Jack's angry look, she realized she hadn't told him about her roommate. "Yeah, he's one of my oldest friends. He's an artist, too, a sculptor. In high school we lived across the street from each other. And he used to drag me to every second-rate horror movie that came out." She knew she was babbling, but she couldn't stop herself. "When we bumped into each other a few years ago, we decided to rent an apartment together."

At that moment her roommate undid the last lock and walked into the living room. With a quick glance, Nathan took in the situation, then flashed her a "We'll have to talk later" look.

"Hello, dear." He elegantly arranged himself in one of the armchairs facing the couch. "Did I overhear you maligning my choice of movies again?"

"Yes, you did. Let me introduce my boss, Jack O'Connor. There was a problem in my classroom at the shelter, and he came over to tell me about it."

The two men exchanged hellos, Jack looking like a giant next to her slight roommate.

Indicating the pizza, Nathan said, "Please, don't let me interrupt your dinner."

"I was just on my way out," Jack said tersely. To her surprise, he stood, an artificial smile tacked on his face. "Thanks for the pizza and the beer, Wendy."

"Sure you can't stay for a cup of coffee?" she asked. Or another long, even more passionate kiss?

Nathan smiled impishly. "Perhaps a little Drambuie?"

"No, thank you both."

She could almost swear that Jack was uneasy. But about what, she couldn't be sure.

Turning to her, he gave her one of his cool, unreadable looks. "See you at the shelter tomorrow."

"You bet. I'll be there at nine to help with the cleanup." Before he could say no, she put up her hand. "I insist."

"See you then. Good night." He strode out the door and down the hall.

"Good night," she said to his back. Watching until he got in the elevator, she felt bereft.

What had just happened? Had he been upset because she had a male roommate? No, surely she'd made it clear that Nathan wasn't her boyfriend. Why, then, had Jack bolted? Had he been turned off because her roommate was gay? No, a man who sheltered homeless teenagers seemed likely to be more tolerant than that.

Maybe she was wrong about Jack's attraction to her. Maybe he liked her well enough, but the kiss hadn't been any big thing for him. God, what a depressing thought.

"Aren't you going to close the door?" Nathan came to stand next to her, eyeing her with concern.

"Oh, yeah, right," she said flatly, slamming the door, then mechanically heading toward the hallway that led to her room.

"Do you want to talk about it?"

"About what?" She turned to look at her friend.

He wrinkled his nose. "Don't be obtuse, darling. About the electricity that was sparking between you and that tall, dark man you're working for." His voice changed and became more tender. "It's obvious something happened."

"We had a wonderful, passionate kiss, then as soon as you came home, he just about ran out."

"And you don't know why, do you?" He gave her an affectionate pat on the shoulder. "Sweetie, it's obvious he likes you a lot. Maybe he's got some problem—like another girlfriend or something—that you don't know about. Try not to take it personally."

"That sounds like good advice. It's been a long day, Nate. I'm going to bed."

"Sleep tight. Don't let the bedbugs bite."

Five

As he walked to his car, Jack hunkered down in his sheepskin jacket, bracing himself against the cold wind that blew down from Twin Peaks. He grimaced. His virginity was an albatross around his neck. It was similar to trying to get a job without any prior experience: You couldn't get the job without the experience, and you couldn't get the experience without the job.

He opened the door to his ten-year-old white American Motors car—his kids called it the "Narcmobile"—then climbed into the front seat. For a moment he just sat there, watching a thick blanket of fog wrap itself around the old warehouses dotting the South of Market area. The fog—ghostly and beautiful—shrouded the night; he shivered against its dampness.

After switching on the ignition, he cranked up the heater. Things had started off so well this evening. Although he hadn't gone to Wendy's apartment with the intention of kissing her, the moment they touched, it had seemed so natural. He hoped she hadn't noticed his heart pounding like the surf at Baker Beach.

Absentmindedly he ran his hand along the curve of the steering wheel, recalling the texture of her silky skin, the sweetness of her warm lips against his. The heat between them had begun to build, threatening to engulf them. Then Nathan had showed up.

When Jack tried to recapture that sense of being connected to Wendy, he couldn't hold on to it; it vanished, slipping through his fingers like the white, bodiless fog outside the window. Putting the car in gear, he drove off down the street.

He parked in the lot next to the Church of St. Evangeline, where Father Quinn was monsignor. Even though it was nearly midnight, a yellow light burned in the cramped, tidy office at the back of the rectory. Father Quinn smiled when he saw him, pushing aside the stack of files on his desk and pocketing his wire-rimmed glasses.

"Ah, Jack! You haven't paid me this many visits in a long time." He eyed the young man speculatively, then glanced at his watch. "You know, I'm feeling a little hungry. Shall we grab a bite to eat?"

"Just what I had in mind," Jack said, ignoring the rumblings of the pizza in his belly. "Mexican okay with you?"

Father Quinn's eyes lit up. "Perfect! This is just the sort of night for spicy food. Warms the belly *and* the soul."

Jack drove to his favorite Mexican food joint, Miguel's 24-Hour Taco Stand and Gas Station. The neon lights of the restaurant sign reflected off the shiny black hair of two young lovers at the counter. Hunched over on orange plastic stools, the couple exchanged soft words and touches. Jack added salsa to his beef burrito and wished Wendy were by his side.

Father Quinn munched contentedly on his taco. "How are the kids at the shelter?"

"Fine." Jack's mind raced back to Wendy. How could he have been so forward with a woman he hardly knew? Had he insulted her—or worse yet, revealed his inexperience—and turned her off? He must have seemed rude to her roommate, Nathan, when he'd left so hurriedly. Jack cringed inwardly. Not exactly one of his shining moments. How he hated this feeling of incompetence!

Father Quinn added a generous dollop of guacamole to his beans and rice. "And how are you?"

"Fine, too." Jack pushed aside his half-eaten burrito and wrapped his cold hands around his warm paper coffee cup. He hoped he hadn't irretrievably damaged his relationship with Wendy.

Across from him, Father Quinn sat silently, waiting, his black eyes wise and warm. A master of eliciting confessions, the priest wouldn't ask probing questions unless Jack volunteered some information.

Looking out across the parking lot at the rows of revamped Cadillacs with their polished chrome bumpers, Jack said, "See those cars out there?"

"Yes."

"When I look at them, I see the hours, the time, the attention, the money, that have gone into them. And I ask myself, for what?"

Father Quinn considered the cars and his answer. "They must give their owners a sense of pride, accomplishment, perhaps even power."

Jack took a sip of his hot coffee. "Yeah. But was it worth it? When you're done, all you have is a cold car. It can't keep you warm at night."

"That's true." Father Quinn polished off his second taco and delicately licked his fingers.

"But it's not just cars," Jack said, knowing his voice sounded harsh. He also knew Father Quinn wouldn't take the irritation in his voice personally. "It's that sense that you've been putting your energy in the wrong place. That you've missed the boat somehow."

Father Quinn made an understanding sound.

A memory flashed in Jack's mind. He saw his small room at home, sparsely decorated, not looking like the room of the average teenager. "When I was twelve and decided to become a priest, I shut myself off from other kids my age. My room in my mom's house had no posters, no stereo, just books and papers. Every Friday and Saturday night, I'd escape there to spend my solitary moments. Until being alone and doing things by myself became a habit. I didn't know any other way." Sometimes he wondered if he could break out of the shell he'd spent so many years carefully building around himself. "Now I look back and think, 'What a waste!' "

"Don't dismiss what you've done in the past." The older man

neatly wrapped up his empty plate, plastic fork, and spoon in his paper napkin. "The guy who works on his Cadillac may decide to do something else. But that doesn't change the fact that he worked on, polished, loved that car. He's just ready for a new challenge. And he can take what he learned about himself to his next task."

Jack avoided Father Quinn's eyes; both men looked straight ahead as if there were an invisible wall separating them, the confessional wall that gave the speaker—and the listener—the promise of anonymity.

"I see your point," Jack said, stirring cream into his cloudy coffee. When he was in seminary school, he'd thought that celibacy was the most difficult challenge. Now he watched the two lovers across from him, noting how they leaned together, trusting and opening up to each other. Maybe he'd been wrong. Maybe celibacy was easy compared to intimacy. "I just wonder if it's really possible for people to change."

"God thinks so." Father Quinn's eyes turned to meet his.

Jack smiled without humor. There it was again. A reminder of the problem with his faith. "I wish I had your trust, your ability to believe, without trying to *understand* or control everything."

"The world needs good questioners. You just have to know when there isn't an answer or when you're trying to control what you can't control."

Rubbing his throbbing temples, Jack let the older man's words sink in. That had always been one of his biggest problems: trying to control the uncontrollable. Trying to be the best seminary student possible, trying to run the greatest shelter in the city, trying to direct others with the same firm hand that he used to control himself. And, he was beginning to understand, being involved with another person meant letting go of control. Could he do it?

"This one's on me," Jack said, picking up the check.

The priest looked at the other man's nearly full plate, but made no comment. "You've changed a great deal already," Father Quinn said, gripping Jack's shoulder warmly. "Have faith."

At nine the next morning, Wendy opened the door to her classroom. Although she'd tried to prepare herself for the worst, her stomach sank as she looked at the wanton destruction. She hated seeing the thick puddles of bright paint, the high-quality art paper torn and strewn around the room, and the broken paintbrushes scattered about like so much garbage.

There was a sound in the hall. She turned to see Jack walk in. Dressed in a worn flannel shirt and an old pair of jeans that hugged his firm thighs, he managed to look sexier in work clothes than most men did in a tuxedo. One glance at his face told her that he was in no mood for flirtatious banter. His dark brows were drawn together in a frown across his high forehead, making him look forbidding and unapproachable.

He spoke curtly. "Let's get to work."

Hurt momentarily flashed through her, then pride intervened. She could play distant just as well as the next person. "Sure. What shall we do first?"

They divvied up the chores and worked in strained silence, exchanging only necessary words. She was acutely aware of his presence in the room. At one point, they bent down to pick up the mop and the broom at the same time, and their hands collided. He looked at her, a raw expression of hunger in his dark blue eyes. The breath stilled in her chest and her heart seemed to stop. He looked as if he wanted to touch her again.

"I'm sorry," he said, stepping back.

"It's okay."

His remoteness upset her, particularly after the warm kiss they'd exchanged the night before. Did he regret what had happened, fearing that now she'd expect something from him that he wasn't prepared to give? That was a distinctly unpleasant thought. Having grown up with distracted, workaholic parents, she knew what it felt like to be unwanted, in the way, and nothing more than a bother. Squaring her shoulders, she got back to work.

After another five minutes of unnatural quiet, the tension became too much for her. "Is something bothering you?" she blurted out.

"What do you mean?" He regarded her as if she were speaking in Swahili.

Oh, great! He was making this as hard as possible. Well, what did she have to lose? She'd already said more than she should have. Why not go the distance? "Last night I thought we had a really fun time, but now you're hardly speaking to me. What's going on?"

He ran a hand through his thick, dark hair. His hard look softened and was replaced by an almost tired expression. "I guess I've been acting like a jerk, haven't I?"

"I wouldn't go that far," she said. "You're just confusing me. I'm getting mixed signals."

He seemed to hesitate for a moment, as if he were about to reveal something. Finally he said, "I'm feeling pressured here at work. It's been a tough week—and now this vandalism." He scanned her face, then smiled a real smile. "I didn't exercise this morning. Maybe that's my problem."

She took a chance. "Were you upset because Nathan came home last night and . . . interrupted us?"

"It caught me off guard because I didn't know you had a roommate. But it didn't upset me. I had a great time last night." He extended his hand. "Friends?"

She took his warm, firm hand in hers. "Friends."

The word "friend" didn't encompass the feelings she was starting to have for this enigmatic man, but maybe she'd be wise to keep their relationship platonic. She wasn't sure she wanted to get involved with *anybody* right now—and certainly not with a man who seemed more leery of intimacy than she was.

At that moment, Lamar burst into the classroom. Wendy quickly dropped Jack's hand.

"Hi, teach . . ." Lamar began, then stopped as he saw the damage done to the room. Shock fleetingly registered on his face. Thrusting his hands in his pockets, he drawled, "What happened here? Freddy the Thirteenth pay you a visit?"

She chuckled in spite of herself. The kid had moxie.

"Lamar!" Jack said with uncharacteristic harshness. "You'll address your teacher as Ms. Valdez. You know the rules here."

The boy's mouth dropped open at Jack's tone. For a moment, Wendy saw an image of the lost child Lamar must have been as a young boy. "Yes, sir."

Wendy suspected that Jack was uncomfortable about what happened last night and was taking it out on Lamar.

"This don't mean we're gonna miss class today, does it, Ms. Valdez?" Lamar shifted on his feet.

Looking around her classroom, she made a snap decision. She and the kids needed a clean place to meet, and she wanted to be away from Jack so that she could try to sort out her thoughts.

"We're going on a field trip to my studio, Lamar. We can all fit in my van." She turned to Jack "If that's okay with you, that is."

His dark-fringed eyes examined her face. "What are you going to do there?"

Have pizza and a make-out party, she thought sarcastically. "Show them what an artist's studio is like. Let them see some of my work and Nathan's and the sorts of tools, paints, and brushes we use."

Jack rubbed his hands on his dusty pants. "All right. Just be sure they're back in time for their next class."

"Will do."

"Leave the rest of this mess. I'll get some of the kids to finish cleaning it up." Whatever openness Jack had been feeling was once again submerged beneath his take-charge attitude.

"Thanks."

As she watched him leave the room, she wondered what he was trying so hard to hide. Then she wondered if he ever let anyone get close enough to find out.

Standing in her living room, Wendy watched her students explore their new surroundings. Gillian picked up one of the clean paintbrushes off the coffee table and ran it over her cheek.

"Fresh!" the girl said. "This is softer than my makeup brush! What's it made of?"

"Boar's bristle." Opening her supply box, Wendy showed them the different types of brushes and what they were best suited for.

"This is a hot crib you got." Lamar leisurely strolled over to the large windows that filtered the day's light into the spacious living room. Shooting a sly look at Wendy, he asked, "You live here solo or you got yourself a sugar daddy?"

She schooled her features into a bland expression. "I share the apartment with my roommate, Nathan."

"Ohhh!" Lamar clapped his hands and hooted. "Ms. Valdez has got herself a boyfriend."

"Roommate, not boyfriend. Nathan's an artist, too."

Lamar shot her a disgusted look. "Don't say nothing more. I got the picture. You adults are weird."

"Let me show you some of his work." Leading the way, she

took them into Nathan's room, where several of his latest soft sculptures resided.

Gillian poked her head into a large hot pink sculpture that resembled a twisting tunnel or an undulating worm. "Can I crawl in here?"

"Sure. That's what it's for," Wendy said, affectionately ruffling the girl's blond hair. "A local nursery school commissioned him to build a sculpture that kids could play in."

Without another word, Lamar crawled in after Gillian. Even Pam relented and climbed into the tunnel. The infectious sound of young laughter filled the room. Wendy felt a lump in her throat. How often did they get the chance to just goof off without worrying?

When it was time to leave, Lamar shot a longing look at her apartment. "Not a bad place, teach. Your stuff ain't my style, but it ain't bad."

Smiling at his high praise, Wendy locked the door behind her, then drove her charges back to the shelter.

After dropping the kids off in the care of Mrs. Hughes, Wendy went to the art store and ran some errands. The sun had set by the time she returned home. Tonight her apartment seemed particularly empty. Elsie wasn't back from the vet, the teenagers were all safely back at the shelter, Nathan was out at a party, and she was alone. Normally she cherished her few free moments, but this evening she wished she had someone to keep her company. A tall, dark, enigmatic someone.

She shook her head at the direction in which her thoughts were wandering. Although Jack was definitely handsome and interesting, she had to remember he wasn't her type. She must be lonelier and more frustrated than she wanted to admit.

After dropping her purse and supplies on the couch, she walked into the kitchen to make herself a cup of tea. Then she spotted the graffiti. Large black letters covered her recently pristine white walls. "Valdez is a baybe" and "hot-lipes." She assumed they meant "babe" and "Hot lips." Other words looked like the names of gangs or gang members.

As she looked around the room, she knew one of the kids from the shelter must have done this—just like one of them had vandalized her classroom. But which kid? And why?

She felt a chill as she thought of someone breaking into her apartment. The front door hadn't been forced. How had they come in? Were they still here?

Her heart beating quickly, she picked up her baseball bat and checked all the rooms and closets. Empty.

Relieved, she sank down on one of the tall stools in front of the butcher block table. She had to do something, and fast. This had to stop. Scanning the writing on the walls again, she thought of Jack; he'd know what to do.

With shaky hands, she dialed the number for the shelter. "Jack?"

"Yes?" His voice was solid-sounding, banishing some of her edginess.

She told him about the graffiti. "I'd like to talk to you about it and try to figure out what to do."

"Stay put," he said firmly. "I'll be right over."

Fifteen minutes later, the doorbell rang.

She checked through the peephole. Jack's tall form dwarfed the hallway. The wind had whipped his black hair into charming disorder. Opening the door, she said, "Come in."

He scanned her face. "You look pale."

"I'm in a state of shock."

He put a strong arm around her shoulders and gave her a hug. "We'll straighten this out. Don't worry."

Grateful for his support, she took him into the kitchen, where he silently surveyed the writing on the wall.

"Looks like it was done by one of our kids. Maybe the same person who ransacked your classroom."

She shuddered. "Why? It gives me the creeps."

Again he examined her face. "You shouldn't be here alone right now. I was on my way out for dinner when you called. Why don't you join me?"

Dinner with Jack? Was that a good idea? Probably not, but warm food and his company sounded great just now.

"I'd love to," she said, grabbing her purse and keys.

They were the only customers in the fragrant-smelling French Vietnamese restaurant. It was just after five and the dinner crowd hadn't arrived yet. A slender Asian waitress led them to a table in the back. Another girl floated silently through the room, lighting the candles that sat in the center of each pink tablecloth. From the kitchen at the back came the clank of silverware and the high-pitched trill of feminine laughter.

When they reached their table, Jack pulled out a wooden chair for her. His eyes seemed to scan her face and body with appreciation. Her heart lurched. Until she could get her erratic emotions under control, she was glad they were meeting in a public place.

"This is one of my favorite restaurants," he said, handing her a menu. "I recommend number fourteen." His eyes bored into her with an intensity that she found unnerving.

She forced herself to look down at the menu, trying to concentrate on the exotic dishes the restaurant offered. "What is it?"

"Chicken on fire with mint and peanut sauce."

"Sounds spicy. And delicious." And he looked the same way in the half light of the candle's glow.

"It is. A mix of unexpected flavors."

Wendy caught herself staring at him. She was startled when the waitress's soft, inflected voice asked to take their order.

"We'll start with the spicy beef salad," Jack said. "I'll have number fourteen, and the lady will have . . ." He raised his eyebrows questioningly at Wendy.

"The same. With brown rice."

Smiling, the waitress left them alone.

He shifted his large frame in his chair. "You won't be disappointed that you took a chance."

"I like the unexpected." She felt that they were talking about anything but the meal.

"I thought so."

Every time she was with him, she saw a different aspect of his personality. Last night he'd been playful. This morning, angry and unreachable. And now, he was a dark, brooding presence.

Reaching across the table, he surprised her by taking her hand in a firm grip. "You must be frightened by this vandalism."

"A bit," she admitted. "I'm starting to feel someone has it in for me."

"After working with these kids for several years, my gut sense is that it's not truly dangerous. Illegal, stupid, annoying—yes. Dangerous—probably not." His strong fingers lightly caressed her hand, sending warm tingles along her skin.

"Thanks. I'm glad you don't think I should be too concerned. But we've got to find some way to catch whoever is doing this." As she stared into his blue eyes, inspiration hit. "Wait! I've got an idea."

"What's that?"

"I noticed that 'hot lips' was misspelled. Whoever wrote it spelled it hot l-i-p-e-s."

"Sounds like Lamar," he said.

"Doesn't it? But I want to be sure before I say anything. So I think what I'll do is give a pop spelling quiz in my next class. And then if it's one of the kids in my class, I'll know who."

"Clever." His white teeth glinted in a brief smile. "What will you do when you find out who did the graffiti?"

She took her hand out of his. "I don't know yet. Maybe make him stay after class a few times."

An incredulous look came over his features. "Stay after school for breaking and entering? No, you've got to report this to the police."

"The police! But what if it's just Lamar and he's got a little crush on me? I don't want him to go to jail. He's just a kid."

He gave her a stern look. "Kids can do terrible things. Especially if they think they can get away with it."

"Well, I can't send a kid to jail for writing graffiti."

"First of all, whoever did it will probably get probation, and second—"

She cut him off. "Jack, I won't press charges if it could mean jail time."

"You're making a mistake, but it's your call. At the very least, make whoever did it buy paint and personally repair your kitchen."

For a moment she wanted to insist that he was being too harsh, that it wasn't that serious an incident. Then she remembered how frightened she'd felt when she realized someone had been in her apartment. "Okay," she said. "That sounds reasonable."

At that moment, the waitress brought their steaming, colorful platters. Jack served rice, then ladled out the fragrant entreé. "Tell me what you think."

Taking a bite of the tender chicken, she savored the flavors of peanut butter and mint. "Delicious." She quickly licked a drop of sauce off her lip, then stopped when she saw the look of hunger on his face. "An unusual combination."

He brought a morsel of food to his mouth. "Sometimes those are the best, don't you think?"

Was she imagining things or was he referring to the two of them instead of the cuisine? His dark eyes were opaque in this light, his expression hard to read.

A frisson of uneasiness—or excitement?—moved through her limbs. His innuendos made her uncomfortable. Talking with him was rather like walking through a treacherous bog; she never knew where she could step safely. What was it Dear Abby said about men? "Ask them about themselves." Maybe her questions would extinguish that seductive glint in his gaze. "Tell me, how did you get involved with the shelter?"

"Ever since I was a kid, I wanted to help people." He paused for a moment, his blue eyes taking on a distant look. "My mother had very strong convictions. Early on, she taught me and my two brothers that we had to make a contribution to the community. She always said it wasn't enough to take, you had to give something back."

"Your mother sounds like an intense woman." She watched his face soften, the lines at the edge of his eyes crinkling as he gave a wry smile.

"Yeah. A five-foot-two fireball. My dad was a motorcycle cop— killed on duty when I was five. So my mom raised the three of us by herself—on a nurse's salary."

Wendy felt a rush of compassion for this strong man seated across from her. Although her relationship with her parents was strained at best, at least she hadn't had to face their death. Just thinking about the fact that one day they wouldn't be around caused her pain. "I'm sorry. It must have been hard to lose your father when you were so little."

"It was. All I remember about him is he had a deep laugh, told wonderful stories, and that he had great shoulders for horseback riding. And somehow—even after he was gone—I knew he loved me."

She felt as if a curtain had parted, revealing a part of Jack that he normally kept hidden behind his decisive, no-nonsense personality. "He sounds like a good man."

"He was. My brothers always told me stories about how brave he was and how much he loved his job as a policeman."

"Your brothers are older?"

"Yep. Derek was nine when Dad was killed, and Brian was seven. They're both physicians now."

"Two doctors. That's unusual. Did you ever want to become a doctor?"

"Never." He moved the glass jar that held the candle across the linen tablecloth, causing the light to flicker over his face. "I never wanted to fix people's bodies. I wanted to make them feel better about themselves." As he ran his hands through his hair, his eyes seemed turned to some inner scene. "I've thought about it, trying to figure out where this impulse comes from. And I think it's from my mom."

"How so?"

"When my dad died, I was still a kid, my mom's baby. She tried hard to protect me, so hard, in fact, that I felt I had to be strong for *her.*"

"That's awfully mature for a five-year-old."

"Yes and no. I thought I had to fix her. Make her happy. But I was a kid, so I couldn't do anything. Except listen. Of course, time passed, and she did feel better." He pushed his massive shoulders back against his chair. "Being an egotistical squirt, I thought *I'd* made her better." His blue eyes burned into hers. "The impulse to help has never left me."

She was riveted by the passion and conviction in his tone. It was unusual to find a man who felt this strongly about his work—and who was able to articulate his feelings. She hadn't expected Jack to have an introspective side—or to reveal it to her. Still, she sensed he was leaving something crucial out of his description of himself, some fact that would help her understand him.

"How about your dad? Did you ever want to follow in his footsteps and be a policeman?"

"Sure. When I was real little. Then I figured out that I wanted to make a more lasting impression on someone's life than giving him a ticket—"

"Or sending him to jail?" Spotting a devilish glint in his eyes, she was glad her irreverence hadn't offended him.

"You've got a point. Sending someone to jail is rather permanent." He fell silent for a moment as if searching for words. "I didn't want to police anyone. I wanted to be strong for them when they couldn't be strong themselves—be a doctor of the spirit." He waited while the waitress refilled their water glasses, then shrugged. "Selfishly, I wanted to see my patients get better."

She nodded in understanding. "Thus the shelter."

"Exactly."

Taking a sip of the jasmine tea, she studied the handsome planes of his face. The more she learned about him, the more intrigued she was. "How did you end up working with teenagers?"

He stretched out his long legs. "After my dad died, we had some lean years there—your basic no-frills childhood. My mom almost lost our house a couple of times. We stared at poverty every day, and just managed to keep it outside our door."

"So you can relate to these kids, too." Looking at his austere black outfit and the stark cut of his features, she began to understand the forces that had made him into a driven, dedicated man.

"Yep. I know what it's like to have to grow up before your time. The best thing I can give these kids is what my mom gave me. A sense of purpose and direction."

To her surprise, tears welled up in her eyes; she hoped he couldn't see them. Why did she feel like crying? Was it because his story had reminded her of her parents—and how little interest they'd taken in her as a child? Or did she simply long for the self-confidence that radiated from him? He seemed to know exactly what he wanted from life and how to get it. With a pang, she realized that she had never felt that sort of single-minded commitment to anything. Never.

"Your goals and your drive are admirable."

"Thanks. But don't be too impressed. This isn't a job to me. It's what I love."

A silence fell between them. The waitress came to clear away their empty plates, then handed them the dessert menu.

"Try the coffee drink," Jack said, leaning across the table to point out the item in the menu. "It's a mix of cream and sweet coffee—delicious."

"Sounds fattening."

He gave her a distinctly masculine perusal. "You don't look as if you need to worry."

She felt the hot flush move up her neck and across her cheeks. "Thank you. I'll try the coffee."

"Good." He turned to the waitress "Make it two and a banana fritter." His gaze returned to Wendy. "We'll share."

Feeling embarrassed, she glanced around the room. The restaurant was beginning to fill up. Noisy, happy groups of people sat at nearby tables, destroying the fragile cocoon of separateness that had enveloped the two of them. "This looks like a popular place."

"Yep. Aux Delices is one of my favorite spots. I come here once or twice a week."

"Do you eat out a lot?" she asked.

"Yep. My apartment's near the shelter, but I hardly ever leave work before eight or nine. The last thing I want to do is go home and cook."

He didn't sound as if he had a significant other. "I completely understand," she said. "I have the same relationship to cooking that I do to my vacuum cleaner: I leave it alone and it doesn't bother me."

That prompted him to laugh, a clear, deep sound that made several other women look appreciatively in his direction. "Well, I hate to break this moment of camaraderie, but I like to cook—just not for myself."

She asked, "Where did you learn to cook?"

"It was either that or look at one more frozen entrée and commit hara-kiri."

It was her turn to laugh. "Please, say no more. If I spot another Lean Cuisine in my freezer, I'm getting my Uzi and knocking out the whole machine."

"Look, I make a killer beef stew," he said. "You'll have to come over and try some. How about next Friday?" The unspoken invitation in his eyes did indecent things to her blood pressure.

"Sounds great. What can I bring . . . that can be defrosted?"

He shuddered. "Nothing. Remember, we want something healthy."

"Like beef stew? Think of your heart!"

"Last time I checked, my heart was doing just fine." His expression gave his words a subtle undercurrent. "Besides, we're talking fresh ingredients, lots of vegetables. Good food."

"Enough," she said. "I'm convinced. How about if I bring some sourdough bread and make a salad?"

"It's a deal. Let's say eight o'clock?" After glancing at the tab, he put down some money. "Tonight's my treat."

"Thanks. For dinner and for coming over right away. I didn't want to be alone in my apartment."

"I know." Reaching across the table, he took her hands in his again.

His touch was electric. Wendy tried to act normally as his strong fingers caressed her skin.

He asked, "Do you think Nathan will be back yet?"

"No, he's at a party. He won't be back till late." Was he inviting himself over or was he concerned about her being home alone?

"Do you want me to come over until he gets back?"

Without a doubt, but it probably wasn't a good idea. "Thanks," she said, "but I'll be fine."

"It's still early," he insisted, not letting go of her hands. "We could rent a video, make popcorn, and hang out until Nathan gets back."

"Sounds wonderful."

Even as the words escaped her lips, she wondered if she was ready for this. And what exactly *was* this anyway? A friendship? A romance? A work relationship with social occasions thrown in? A kamikaze mission? Well, whatever it was, she wanted to spend more time in his company, so she'd find out, wouldn't she?

They left the restaurant and drove to a nearby video store. Inside, Wendy picked some recent releases off the shelves. Showing him a couple, she said, "How about one of these?"

"Too slick." He put the video boxes back, then pulled a French comedy off the rack. "This will lift your spirits."

"I hate subtitles."

"It's a very physical comedy. You'll love it. Trust me."

Fifteen minutes later they were back at her apartment. She fixed a big bowl of popcorn. Together they pulled pillows off the sofa and settled themselves on the floor. She dimmed the lights. He sat near her, but not too close.

"Comfortable?" she asked.

"Very." He put a piece of popcorn in his mouth.

She felt a twinge of disappointment. Why was he suddenly acting as if they were brother and sister? One minute he was flirting with her, then they were back in her apartment alone and she might as well be sitting there with Nathan. With an impatient flick of the remote control, she started the movie.

The video was very funny, and despite her irritation, she found herself relaxing. When she reached for popcorn, her hand kept bumping into his.

"We keep doing this, don't we?" She started to laugh, then stopped when she saw the burning light in his eyes.

"Clumsy, aren't we?" he said. For a moment she saw raw hunger in his expression, then he was smiling, as guileless as a choirboy.

She nursed her bottle of sparkling apple juice. Something weird was going on here. Either she was losing her mind, or he was playing some sort of game with her. Every one of her senses told her he was attracted to her, but he kept retreating. What was the guy's problem?

Was he married, but just didn't wear a ring? No, he didn't strike her as that sort of man. Maybe he had a girlfriend? A girlfriend who didn't eat dinner with him or care if he came home late several nights a week? Seemed unlikely. Well, she didn't know what was wrong, but she could sense his reserve again, separating them as firmly as the Berlin Wall used to separate the East and the West.

The more she thought about it, the more she realized that dinner at his place was probably not a good idea. After tonight, she'd have to keep her distance from him. Otherwise, she suspected she'd get hurt.

"How'd you like it?" he asked.

She came out of her reverie to see the end credits rolling up the screen. "Hysterical. Very amusing. The funniest thing I've ever seen." All she wanted to do was get him out of her apartment. She felt like a fool.

He gave her a strange look.

Grabbing the empty popcorn bowl, she jumped up and chirped, "Well, what a pleasant evening! Thank you so much for treating me to dinner and for coming over to keep me company." She knew she was blabbering. She always blabbered when she was hurt or rejected.

He slowly rose to his full height. "My pleasure."

"Nathan should be home any minute. Don't feel you need to stay."

"I'm in no rush—"

"Besides," she hurried on, "I have some work I really need to do." After walking to the door, she pointedly held it open, a bright smile plastered on her face. "Thanks so much for everything. It was very sweet of you to be so concerned."

"Don't mention it." He put his hands into the pockets of his black jeans, unwittingly drawing her eyes to the muscular shape of his legs. What would it be like to feel his hard thighs against her skin?

Get a grip on yourself, girl. These fantasies had to stop. The man was interested in saving the kids in his shelter, good restaurants, and French comedies. She didn't fit on the list.

Again he looked at her as if he wanted to ask what had happened to her mood. Instead, he simply smiled and said a polite good night.

"See you tomorrow. And thanks again." She virtually slammed the door shut behind him and flicked on the locks. Good riddance! Looking at the chairs she still needed to paint, she decided a good, hot soak in the tub was more important. Tomorrow she'd tell Jack that she couldn't join him for dinner after all.

Then she'd let Nathan know she was interested in that blind date.

Six

When Wendy arrived at Valencia House on Tuesday, she studiously avoided Jack's office. Business first, last, and exclusively—that would be her motto when dealing with the unpredictable Mr. O'Connor.

In her classroom, Gillian greeted her with a smile, Pam with a defiant stare, and Lamar with a suspiciously cherubic grin. Wendy put her fishing tackle box on her desk, then silently passed out a stack of papers and pencils.

"Class," she said, "please put your name on the top right-hand side of your paper. We're having a spelling test."

The three kids all groaned out loud at once.

"What!?" Gillian looked surprised. "This is art class, not English."

"Just don't make me spell Picasso," Pam said.

"Spelling?" Lamar croaked. "Did you say 'spelling'?"

Wendy wondered if he could have looked more horrified if she'd suggested torturing small animals.

"Let's get started. The first word is 'paintbrush.' "

Her charges grumbled as they wrote. Casually training her gaze on Lamar, she continued, "The second word is 'hot lips.' "

He gave a guilty start, then buried what sounded like a laugh behind a cough. "This ain't fair, teach. We didn't get no chance to prepare."

She continued dictating, "And the last word is baby."

After waiting a minute, she collected the tests. A quick look revealed that Lamar had misspelled *hot lips* and *baby* in exactly the same way that they had been misspelled on her kitchen walls. *Le voilà,* her graffiti artist.

"Lamar," she said. "Please stay after class."

The young man sullenly tugged on his hairnet, but said nothing.

Gillian shot her a perplexed look. "What's this all about anyway?"

"Forget it." Pam dragged her scuffed black cowboy boots back under her desk. "She ain't gonna tell us."

"Teacher's privilege," Wendy said.

She quickly involved the teenagers in various art projects. Just before class ended, the door opened at the back of the room and Jack walked in.

The sight of his tall, well-made form made her heart pick up its beat. Relax, she told herself. Remember, this guy is the Dr. Jekyll and Mr. Hyde of Romance. Her heart was knocking against her chest out of fear and anxiety—not attraction.

"Hello, class, Ms. Valdez." His eyes twinkled.

She returned his hello, wondering if he was being formal to set an example for the kids or because he wanted to put some distance between them.

The kids sat up straighter in their chairs. "Good afternoon, Mr. O'Connor."

When Jack reached her desk, he leaned toward her and whispered conspiratorially, "How'd the spelling test go?"

"Very revealing." She kept her voice light and friendly. Although normally she didn't edit her emotions, something about the intensity of her feelings for Jack made her cautious. "As we suspected, it was Lamar. He's staying for a little chat after class."

"Good work, detective." He scanned her face. "I'll be here to back you up when you talk with him."

"Wonderful," she said, hoping her lack of enthusiasm wasn't too obvious. Jack didn't seem to notice anything odd. Of course not. People who were warm one minute, then cold the next, probably seemed perfectly normal to Mr. Mercurial himself.

Wendy dismissed the rest of the class. Turning to Lamar, she said, "So do you want to tell us why you broke into my studio and wrote graffiti on the wall?"

"Who says I did?"

She opened her purse and took out a Polaroid photo of the damage to her kitchen and held it next to Lamar's spelling test with the misspelled words circled. "This says you did."

"That don't prove nothing. Lot of kids can't spell."

She and Jack regarded Lamar without saying a word until, finally, the teenager sat up angrily in his chair.

"Okay, okay, so I did it. Big deal. What are you gonna do about it? Throw me out on the street?" He laughed derisively. "I ain't afraid of that. I ain't afraid of *nothin'* you two can do to me."

Wendy watched the slender young man cross his arms over his chest, his face schooled not to betray what she knew had to be a frightening concern: going back out on the street. Doubt assailed her. Was she doing exactly the wrong thing by confronting him like this?

Before she could respond, Jack spoke. "No, we're not going to throw you out. That would be too easy. I wanted to report you to the police, but Ms. Valdez convinced me to give you one more chance."

She couldn't help feeling that Jack had taken the lead as if she couldn't handle the situation.

Lamar's body visibly relaxed, but his expression remained impassive. "What do I gotta do?"

Jack turned to her. "I'll let Ms. Valdez tell you."

Forcing herself to sound firm, she said, "You have to buy some paint and repair my kitchen."

"But, Ms. Valdez—"

She held up her hand. "I know you don't have much money. So I've figured out a way that you can work off the cost of the paint." Taking a slip of paper from the pocket of her purple linen jacket, she said, "I called the paint store. Let's see. A can of stain-killer primer and a gallon of latex paint goes for about twenty-eight or thirty bucks. Divide that by four dollars an hour and you get around seven and a half hours."

"Who's gonna give me a job? I ain't working at McDonald's."

"Me. I'll buy the paint and you can pay me back. I have odd jobs around here and at my studio that need doing."

"But, teach, my classes . . ."

"We'll work that out—" she began when Jack interrupted.

"Lamar, you'll go over *today* and paint Ms. Valdez' kitchen."

Her temper began to simmer. She wished he'd let her speak for herself.

"And you'll work off those hours within the next two weeks," Jack continued, his mouth drawn in a firm line. "Or you'll have me to answer to."

"All right, Mr. O'Connor. When we gonna go to your studio, Ms. Valdez?"

"I'll be leaving in a little bit," she said. "I'll find you."

"Okay." The teenager paused awkwardly at the door. "I, um, I'm sorry."

"That's okay—" she started to say, when Jack silenced her by putting his hand on her arm.

"Actions speak louder than words, Lamar. Prove it."

The teenager closed the door quietly on his way out.

Jack turned to her, approval in his eyes. "You handled that really well."

"Then why did you keep overriding me?" she snapped.

"What?"

"One minute you're telling me to handle it my way, then the next minute you cut me off and jump all over Lamar."

"I was trying to help." He sounded surprised at her vehemence. "You're a soft touch with these kids."

"And you're a battering ram. Lamar said he was sorry. You didn't need to give him a sermon."

"He needs to do a lot more than say he's sorry. No one's ever demanded that he be as good as I *know* he can be." Taking a seat across from her, Jack smiled, an indulgent gleam in his eyes.

That ticked her off even more. "I wish you wouldn't smile at me as if I were an amusing two-year-old! It was *my* studio that was broken into by one of *my* students." She tried to regain control of herself and silence the voice of the fishwife who had inexplicably taken over her body. "I know you're just trying to help, but this was my problem to solve." She began to pace the room.

"All I did was give Lamar a time frame to get the work done. Otherwise he would've tried to weasel out of—"

"Like I said," she said in clipped tones, "it was my problem."

"You're being very stubborn." A hard look came over his face. "While I admire your compassion, weakness is a big mistake with these kids."

She stopped in her tracks and stared at him. "You equate compassion with weakness?"

His eyes were like two blue lights on a huge glacier. "When it stops you from doing what's right for one of the kids under *my* care, you bet I do."

The gauntlet had been thrown. "I know this is your shelter and that you understand these kids better than I do—"

"I'm happy to hear that," he said curtly.

She hadn't meant to offend him, but she had to stand up for what she believed in. "We had a deal. You were going to give me a month to try out my teaching methods to see if they work."

"You're talking about two different things. Teaching methods and discipline problems When we made our deal, I didn't expect someone to vandalize your classroom and your studio."

"Neither did I. But I have to treat my kids the same way in class or out of class. And that's with respect."

If eyes could truly shoot daggers, she knew she'd be pinned to the back wall by his glare. "Letting kids get away with things doesn't show them respect—it shows that you don't think they can do better."

She came to stand in front of him. "Who said I was letting Lamar get away with anything?"

"You were going to let him off the hook, weren't you?"

Damn his perceptive powers. "Yes."

"That would have been a mistake."

"I disagree," she said stubbornly. "The important thing is that he said he was sorry."

He crossed his arms and leaned back in his chair. "I think we're at an impasse."

She wanted to take back what she'd said, wanted to extinguish the angry glint in his eyes, but it was time to put their cards on the table. "What do you suggest we do about it?"

"You have the rest of this month to try out your teaching methods, but I reserve final say about discipline problems."

"Okay." What could she say? He *was* the boss. Even if he was dead wrong.

There was an awkward silence as they both regarded each other. She tried to remember when she'd met a man who could make her melt one moment, then send her into a rage the next. They touched off sparks in each other—there was no doubt about it. Too bad the passion he stirred in her would never be tested; they were so utterly incompatible. She found his harshness with the kids off-putting, and he thought she was a wuss. So be it.

Picking up her purse and tackle box from the desktop, she said, "I'm going to go find Lamar."

Jack opened the door for her and waited until she walked out. She stole a glimpse at his expression, but it was undecipherable.

"See you later," he said coolly.

Wendy shrugged, then walked down the hall. What was it about him that brought out the most immature parts of her personality?

Seven

Jack watched Wendy walk away. Why had she been so determined to see his attempts to help as interference? She had all the empathy in the world for her students, but she cut him no slack at all. She only let him get so close, then she pushed him away.

Running his hand through his unruly hair, he tried to pinpoint why she was so appealing to him. She was warm and compassionate—and he valued that in anyone. Having spent years preparing for the priesthood, he looked for individuals who wanted to help people and causes outside of themselves. But that wasn't all.

As he watched Wendy storm down the hall, her jeans clinging to her rounded bottom, he admitted that her sensuality was hardly a liability. She awoke the wild man inside of him, the raw, untamed self who had rebelled against the limitations of the priesthood. His responses to her taught him things he hadn't known about himself.

Sometimes the speed with which he was changing left him feeling uneasy, out of control. But then, whoever said growth was painless?

He headed toward his office. What was he going to do about his feelings for her? It was too soon to tell her how he felt. Yet his attraction kept getting stronger, threatening his ability to function normally. His mind darted back to the night in her apartment. She'd seemed surprised—even unnerved—when he'd taken off after their first kiss. Shaking his head, he grimaced. Since she had no way of knowing that he was a virgin, she probably thought he was just a terrible kisser. Or a first-class jerk.

Stopping at his secretary's desk, Jack scanned the detailed calendar Mrs. Hughes kept for him. A note on his schedule leapt out at him. Could this be the answer to his prayers?

"That's right," he mused out loud. "Today's the day the counselor comes to talk to the girls about love, sex, and marriage. Great! Is the counselor here yet?"

"She arrived about ten minutes ago." Mrs. Hughes delicately tapped a postage stamp on an envelope. "I hear she's very good. Helps the teenagers learn to handle their romantic feelings."

His mind raced. How to handle romantic feelings. What a wonderful idea. Turning on his heel, he headed out of the office.

Mrs. Hughes's surprised voice followed him. "Where are you going?"

"I'll be sitting in on the group for a while," he called over his shoulder. "Hold my calls."

When he entered the lounge, several pairs of eyes turned in his direction. Six girls sat sprawled on the comfortable sofas and armchairs. At the head of the group, a middle-aged woman with deeply sunken eyes sat cross-legged on a pile of pillows.

"Hello." When she smiled, her ivory skin stretched across her features like the finest parchment. "I'm Mrs. Woolf. And you are?"

He introduced himself and told her he'd like to observe the session. "If you don't mind."

Mrs. Woolf turned to the girls. "Would you feel able to express yourself freely if Mr. O'Connor sat in?"

Oh, dear, a touchy-feely woman left over from the sixties, Jack thought.

"No prob'," Gillian said. "Mr. O'Connor's mega trustworthy."

"Yeah, unlike other men," Pam said laconically.

He felt a rush of pride that these girls trusted him. The program wasn't perfect, but it worked.

"Please have a seat, Mr. O'Connor." Mrs. Woolf pointed to an empty armchair at the edge of the circle. "I've asked the young women to tell me what sorts of things they like and dislike in young men. Let's get back to our discussion."

He lowered himself into the chair.

"Okay, like I was saying," Gillian said, flipping her blond hair and popping her gum. "I think it's really gross when a guy is making goo-goo eyes at me, and I *know* he likes me, but he's too much of a wimp to say anything."

Jack stiffened inside. Had he made "goo-goo eyes" at Wendy? Probably. He winced inwardly. How could she miss the fact that he was often staring at her? Maybe he should bite the bullet and tell her he was attracted to her.

"I hear you, girl." A tall black teenager named LaTisha crossed her legs, then shook her shoulders in a gesture of disgust. "The dude ain't getting *nowhere* if he be waiting on *me* to make the first move. I mean, what am I supposed to do, read his feeble mind?"

The girls guffawed.

Jack settled back in his chair, feeling better. The teenagers were right. Honesty was the best policy. It worked in other relationships; why not romantic ones? His mind began to wander. Maybe tonight he'd take Wendy out to dinner and tell her his feelings for her. He wouldn't tell her he was a virgin. Not yet. But he would make that first move. That was the key.

His thoughts were interrupted by LaTisha's voice.

"But I got another one for you, girlfriend." LaTisha leaned forward in her armchair, her brown eyes sparkling. "You want to know what's the worst? When they won't shut up. They be going on about how pretty you are, how they want to be with you for the rest of their lives. Like a Hallmark valentine. I hate that worse than the silent type."

"For real!" said Juanita, a tiny girl with dimples. "I want a man with some mystery, who keeps me guessing. Now, that's romantic."

Mystery, huh? He sank lower in his chair. How could he be honest and mysterious at the same time? Maybe he could show up at Wendy's studio, dressed in a Lone Ranger outfit, and not tell her why. That would be mysterious—if not downright odd. This whole romance game was incomprehensible. It made learning Latin seem like child's play.

Mrs. Woolf addressed the group. "Some very good sharing, girls. Now let's imagine what you'd like in a good relationship. How would you like to be treated by a boy you found special?"

Jack leaned forward in his chair. Here was the real question.

A dreamy look came over Gillian's features. "He could bring me chocolates. As many as I could eat. And flowers. A whole room full."

"Stuffed animals," said a hefty girl named Sally, shaking her scruffy red hair out of her eyes. "He could give me a soft, really adorable teddy bear."

LaTisha spoke next. "Forget that piddly stuff. Take me to a fancy restaurant with white tablecloths, waiters all dressed up in black and white outfits, and a French name on the door. And he can pick me up in a limousine."

"Oh, yeah!" several girls chimed in approvingly.

He smiled to himself. Okay, he could get chocolates, flowers, limousines. They were a little trite, but maybe they would appeal to Wendy. Although he could see her appreciating something more exotic and personal, like a special raspberry vinegar. Ah, but she didn't cook, did she? Maybe a bottle of silky bubble bath; he could go to her studio, fix her bath, massage the tight muscles in her neck, wash her pink-tipped toes, then let his hand trail up the sun-kissed skin of her . . . He stopped himself. He had to remember where he was.

Mrs. Woolf smiled indulgently. "Those are all *things*. How do you want to be treated? Emotionally."

Again Jack listened carefully. Granted, these teenagers hardly represented the mainstream of American womanhood, but they *were* female. This was his best shot to see into a woman's mind.

Juanita volunteered first. "Treat me nice. Listen to me. Be sweet—"

"Respect," LaTisha interjected. "He's gotta let me be who I am, not try to make me be like some chick he wants me to be."

Gillian pondered the question for a moment. "He can't be pushy, try to get me into bed on the first date—"

"No copping feels!" LaTisha giggled.

"Right," Gillian said firmly. "He's gotta let me take my time."

Be patient. Wait. Jack was good at that. Maybe he'd take Wendy to Baker Beach on a warm day. They'd sit on a picnic blanket, and he'd be sweet, tender, caring and non-threatening. The sea breeze would blow through her auburn curls, the sun would warm their skin, and the white clouds would scud across the azure horizon. Pretty soon she'd be driven into a frenzy by his seemingly endless ability to wait; she'd reach over and rub her hands down the skin on his chest, twirling the black hair that grew there. Her eyes would be fevered with passion. She'd lean her lovely body against his and slip her hand under the edge of his trunks. . . .

Jack was snapped out of his dream by a snort from Juanita.

"No way," she said emphatically. "If I like a guy, he's gotta figure that out by himself. Be a man, make the first move. Now, that's a turn-on."

"Oh, la la. Sexy." LaTisha laughed.

Being assertive was a turn-on, was it? Jack saw himself going to Wendy's apartment unannounced, rapping on the door. She would answer in a flimsy nightgown. Before she could say hello, he would pull her into his arms. Giving her a passionate kiss, he would pick her up and carry her to her room, where he'd gently but inexorably push her back down on her bed, run his hands under her silky nightgown, up her taut calves and thighs. . . .

Then, as she began screaming at him for breaking into her apartment, he would explain that he was new at this and just following the suggestions of several teenage girls.

Scratch that fantasy.

Jack sat back in his seat, mentally tossing up his hands. Each girl wanted something different from a man. Be honest. Be mysterious. Be respectful. Stake your territory. Let the woman take her time. He was more confused than when he'd entered the room.

All he wanted to do was find a way to get Wendy alone, remove her clothes piece by piece, then place kisses along that lovely, smooth skin of hers. . . .

What was happening to him? His mind was out of control! He had to get a grip on himself.

"That was very good, girls. We'll talk more next week." Mrs. Woolf turned to Jack. "I hope you found our meeting enlightening, Mr. O'Connor."

About as illuminating as a candle in a windy mine shaft. "Very much. Thanks for letting me sit in."

He studied the faces of the girls around him, seeing the youth and early disappointments etched on their features. It was a good guess that they'd rarely—if ever—been treated with respect by anyone, let alone by a man. Yet they hadn't given up or lost their romantic dreams. Why should he be any less courageous? Or foolish?

When Wendy stepped off the elevator, she spotted Lamar hunched over in front of her door. Fifteen minutes earlier she'd gone to pick up some sandwiches, leaving him painting over the kitchen. Had he gotten locked out somehow?

Shifting the grocery bag she carried to one hip, she pulled out her keys. As she neared her apartment, she saw Lamar painting elegant and surprisingly professional-looking letters that spelled out her name and Nathan's on the wooden door.

"I only asked you to paint the kitchen—" She stopped short when she saw the excited look in Lamar's brown eyes dim as if some light had been extinguished.

"Gotcha, teach."

"Don't get me wrong," she said quickly, taking a closer look at the still wet letters. "You've done a beautiful job here. I just don't want you to feel you *have* to do more than I asked."

Hope came back to his face. "Do you really like it?"

"I do. I think you're quite talented." An idea came to her, and she blurted it out before she lost her nerve. "In fact, how'd you like to design the invitation for an art show Nathan and I are having in a couple of weeks?"

"Wow! That'd be fresh!" Lamar's enthusiasm bubbled up and spilled over in a little dance. "I'll even do some furniture."

Impetuously she gave him a hug. "You're special, kiddo."

"Really?" He got a distinctly adult look in his eyes. "I knew you'd come around."

She quickly let go. "That's not what I meant. Now, back to work."

"Can't blame a guy for trying."

She thought of Jack and wished her life were a little less complicated. Here she had an oversexed fifteen-year-old interested in her, while she couldn't figure out what was going on with Jack O'Connor.

"When you're done painting," she said, "come inside. I bought some lunch for Nathan and us."

"It's a deal." He turned back to his painting, a look of absorption and intensity on his face unlike any she'd seen before. "Just let me finish my masterpiece first."

On Thursday morning as soon as the center opened, Jack began to hear rumors about the furniture Lamar was making at Wendy's studio, about her popularity with her students, and about the growing enrollment in her art class.

"Things are going so well," Mrs. Hughes said, setting a fresh cup of coffee on his desk. "Ms. Valdez has found something the teenagers really like. And with the nature trip planned for next month, they'll have another new experience."

"The nature trip!" He stirred his coffee. "I'd forgotten about that." The weekend trip had been planned months before Wendy started to teach at the shelter. "I need to check out the arrangements in Mendocino before I can take the kids. . . ." His voice trailed off as the idea of taking Wendy along insinuated itself into his mind.

"Why not take Ms. Valdez with you?"

He shot his assistant a dark look. "Are you trying to be a matchmaker, Thelma?"

"Of course not. But it wouldn't hurt you to get involved with a nice young woman like—"

"Thanks, but I can take care of my romantic relationships by myself." And if he couldn't, that was his problem to solve.

After Mrs. Hughes left, he decided to shoot some baskets to clear his mind. The sun was bright as he stepped out onto the courtyard behind the shelter. He'd stripped off his shirt and had worked up a good sweat when the door opened. Wendy came out, dressed in a short purple skirt and cropped jacket. She looked cool and sexy. The sunlight made her hair shine and her bare, tanned legs gleam.

"Mrs. Hughes said you wanted to see me," she said.

He groaned inwardly, then surrendered. Why fight Mrs. Hughes when she was right? "Yeah." Catching the ball, he held it at his side. "I wanted to ask you to come with me on a one-day trip to Mendocino. Next month, I'm taking the kids up there to go camping. First I have to check out accommodations and trails. I could use your input." He wiped the sweat off his brow. "And your company."

Wendy found herself smiling at his uncharacteristic openness. She knew she shouldn't go because he'd been so unpredictable, yet she wanted to. What was that song from *Oklahoma,* "I'm Just a Girl Who Can't Say No?" Why did she have no control over herself when he was around?

"Okay. Sure." She watched the play of the muscles in his back and arms as he made another perfect basket. "When are you going?"

"Tomorrow."

"Friday? Does that mean we forget about dinner?"

"Yeah." He gave her a rakish smile. "I'll treat you to a picnic lunch instead. It takes about two and a half hours to drive up there, so we need to leave early. Around six A.M. I want to rent a canoe and paddle up the estuary a few miles."

"Sounds great." She pulled her mind away from wondering how it would feel to run her hand over his firm biceps. "What can I bring?"

"Something to drink. I'll pick you up about quarter to six."

A ripple of excitement moved through her at the thought of spending a day alone with him. No kids to watch, no class to teach, no Nathan to interrupt their time together. She found herself wondering how Jack would treat her this time. Who would be her traveling companion: Dr. Jekyll or Mr. Hyde?

Wendy rubbed her eyes as Jack drove across the Golden Gate Bridge. God, she hated being up early in the morning. When she'd accepted his invitation, she'd conveniently forgotten that she was an owl, not a lark. At this time of day, it was simply indecent to be anywhere but curled under her comforter and deep in a dream.

She glanced at Jack. His lean, handsome face looked irritatingly chipper. Dark blue eyes scanned the road as he maneuvered his car through the traffic. Like everything else he did, he drove with confidence and intensity.

He took his eyes off the road for a moment. "How are you feeling this morning?"

"Mmmm," she mumbled. Talking was not really an option at six-fifteen A.M.

"That good, huh?"

She heard the teasing note in his voice. Why did morning people get such a sadistic thrill out of tormenting those civilized humans who preferred to sleep to a semi-normal hour?

Gesturing in the direction of the backseat, he said, "There's a thermos of coffee, mugs, and some muffins behind you. Help yourself."

Java! A beam of light pierced the gloom that hung over her head. *"Wunderbar!* How do you take yours?"

"Cream, two sugars."

The only thing she could fault him for was not bringing an I.V. She poured them each a steaming cupful, then took a bite out of a blueberry muffin.

He sipped his coffee. "Are you always this grumpy in the morning or is this a special occasion?"

"I was up till three last night. Painting."

He scanned her face, an amused glint in his eyes. "When you knew we were leaving at six A.M.?"

"I had work to do for my show." She cupped her hands around the warm mug. Landing a spot in the upcoming show had been a big coup for Nathan and her; she wanted to do her best work.

"Relax," he said, turning his eyes back to the road. "We've got a two-and-a-half-hour drive. Why don't you go to sleep?"

"Say no more." She finished her coffee, then curled up in the front seat. Closing her eyes, she sighed contentedly as the black safety net of sleep enveloped her. Maybe he wasn't such a sadist after all. At least he wasn't going to hold her hostage to a barrage of A.M. chitchat.

The sun was warm when Wendy stirred and stretched against the surprisingly cramped feel of her bed. Looking around her, she saw Jack. Panic seized her. What was he doing in her bed? And why was he holding a steering wheel? Surreptitiously wiping the drool off the car seat, she blinked several times. Through the car window she saw the morning sun glinting off the blue waves of the ocean. Mendocino. That's right. They were on their way to Mendocino. Okay, the world was beginning to make sense again.

"Hello, sleepyhead." His voice was sultry as he followed the curves of the road. "You make the most delicious sounds while you're snoozing."

She prayed to God she hadn't been snoring. "Oh, really?"

"Yes, little coos and sighs." He cocked a dark eyebrow at her. "I wondered what you were dreaming."

She'd been dreaming about that kiss they'd exchanged a few nights before. In her dream, the kiss had gone on, deepening and becoming slower, more sensual, more . . . "It's all a blur."

"Then why the seductive smile?" His hand reached out and imprisoned hers.

Savoring the warm, rough feel of his fingers rubbing her hand, she suppressed the urge to giggle. Giggle? The last time she'd giggled had been in high school. "I've got heartburn."

"Yeah, and my name's Sally."

"Well, Sally, are we almost there?"

"As a matter of fact, we are." Releasing her hand, he pointed to a sign on the side of the highway that said CANOE RENTALS. After turning down a gravel-covered incline, he drove past the large grounds of a majestic inn to a bluff where he parked the car. They climbed out.

Stepping to the edge, Wendy looked down at the river and a small dock with a wooden shack at one end and rows of upside-down canoes at the other. On closer inspection, she saw that the river was actually an estuary. To the left, it flowed beneath a large highway overpass, then opened to kiss the sea, which crested white against the blue sky. In the other direction, the sparkling band curved inland through lush reeds and green forests.

"How beautiful!" she exclaimed.

"This is Big River." He took her hand as they walked down a steep flight of wooden steps that led to the landing. "It's a protected estuary that goes several miles inland."

Waving hello to a man and a teenager on the dock, Jack went to sign out a canoe, life jackets, and paddles and to discuss arrangements for the upcoming group trip. Wendy walked to the edge of the weathered landing. Bending down, she watched sunlight dance on the water and listened to the thump of canoes hitting together. After a few minutes, Jack and the other man approached her.

The middle-aged man handed them orange life vests. "Now, remember, Big River's a tidal river for the first eight miles, so plan to start back here before three-thirty. Otherwise, you'll be paddling against the tide—which ain't fun. And if you wait till afternoon tide's done, you'll get stuck coming back in the dark."

Wendy felt a ripple of fear. Nature had always scared her. The thought of being stranded in a canoe up a wild estuary was not her idea of a fun time. Jack helped her into the canoe, then sat in front of her, facing forward.

The canoe operator clenched a cigarette in his yellowed teeth. "We close at five. If you're not back, you'll have to pay for a second day."

"Jack." She nervously cleared her throat. "This is a simple little canoe trip, right? A safe trip. We're not going to get lost or anything. . . ."

"Don't worry. It's under control." Jack took the picnic basket from the canoe operator and tucked it under the seat.

With an oar, the man pushed them away from the dock. As the water slapped against the side of the craft, she swallowed and tried to enjoy the gorgeous scenery. After all, what was the worst that could happen? They could tip over and she'd drown. Or maybe she'd just get wet, catch pneumonia, and then die. Slowly. Or perhaps she'd get attacked by a pack of wild ferrets or whatever else lived in these untamed forests. Nothing to worry about. Unless the ferrets were rabid. It was under control.

"Hello?" Jack's voice penetrated the fog she was in. "Anybody home?"

"Yes, what? Sorry, I was just thinking."

He looked over his shoulder, a smile tugging at the edge of his mouth. "You have to put your paddle in the water, unless you were expecting to be towed up the river."

"Righto." She copied exactly what he'd done. The boat tilted unnervingly to one side.

"Hold it, hold it," he said. "Put your paddle in the other side so we can work together. Without capsizing."

"Of course."

This was terrible. He was going to wish he'd never brought her along. At which point they'd be in sync, because *she* fervently wished she hadn't come. Yes, she wanted to spend time with Jack, but someplace on land, preferably with four walls, central heating, and a microwave. She couldn't remember the last time she'd been out in nature. Maybe it had been the high school sleep-away when Ricky Jarvis had chased her around the campfire and right into a bumper crop of poison oak.

They began to paddle, the oars slipping in and out of the blue water with small splashes. Together, she and Jack began to find a rhythm. The sun beat down on her back and head, causing her body to relax. She watched his proud carriage as he pulled his paddle through the limpid water.

"You okay back there?" His hearty voice sounded wonderful against the lulling gurgles of the river.

"Great." She was surprised to find that she meant it. "This is really great."

Soon they rounded a bend, and the shoreline was no longer visible. Sand banks gave way to underbrush. They floated through a rich green world of trees, reeds, and rushes. Looking down, she could make out the mossy fingers of plants that swayed and waved in the clear water. Overhead, the cries of great blue herons rang clear in the air as they flew from tree limb to tree limb.

Transfixed by the raw beauty that surrounded her, she said, "I don't think I've ever seen color combinations this exquisite before."

"Mother Nature's the best painter of all." Resting his paddle for a while, he let the incoming tide push them up the river. "The kids will love this place. Last time I came here, I left feeling renewed and full of energy."

"I have a confession to make." Dipping her hand into the cool water, she let it slide over her fingers. "I'm not a big nature person. In fact, I was nervous about coming here today."

"No!"

"It sounds silly, but I don't know what's in these waters—"

"Fish. Plants."

"Or what dangerous animals are lurking in the woods—"

"Look! Up ahead!" He put his hand on her arm.

She looked where he was pointing. A doe and her fawn paused

tentatively at the bank. Head elegantly raised to the wind, the doe sniffed, then flashed away into the undergrowth with her baby.

"Okay, so Bambi's not a threat. You know what I mean."

His smile was warm and dark and utterly unnerving. "Relax. Today I'm your guide. Let this place weave its spell."

The sun was high in the sky when she felt another call of Nature.

"Jack, I need to . . . stop for a few minutes."

"Gotcha. Me, too." He steered the canoe into the slippery mud at the side of the river until it stuck. "Ladies first." Turning his back, he crossed his arms.

Gingerly she stepped out of the canoe and onto the mud-covered roots and rocks, nearly losing her footing. Checking to make sure he wasn't looking, she hastily lowered her pants. Suddenly the canoe started to slide back into the water.

"Wait!" She tried to tug her pants up and keep her footing at the same time, but her tennis shoes slipped out from underneath her. With an indelicate plop, she landed in the soft mud on her just barely covered bottom.

Jack paddled the canoe back, then reached out for her. "Are you okay?"

"Just fine. Absolutely fine." She took his hand and stood up carefully, wiping off the mud from her jeans as best she could.

He started chuckling. "I shouldn't laugh, but you look so disgruntled."

"It's okay."

"When we find a place to stop for lunch, you can wash off," he said, helping her into the canoe.

Pivoting away, she let him take his turn. He didn't even have to get out of the boat.

They continued paddling upstream. The sun moved higher in the sky. After an hour, Wendy spotted a small wooden cabin that looked surprisingly intact on the south bank. Curtains hung in the window and piles of wood flanked the door.

She lifted her damp curls off her neck, trying to get some relief from the heat. "Does anybody really live up here?"

"Probably a ranger or some other park employee." Unbuttoning his shirt, he fanned air on his tanned skin and the dark hair that dusted his broad chest.

"I've got to stop paddling for a while. My arms are killing me."

Besides, she wanted to wash off some of the mud. Then maybe Jack would take off his shirt completely and they could prance around nude in the warm sun. She shook her head. "Sunstroke and lack of food are making me a little spacy."

"We'll stop soon," he said. "If I remember correctly, there's a sandy beach up around the next bend where we can have our picnic."

Several minutes later, they tied the canoe to a tree. Jack spread a plaid blanket on the grass. He turned and looked at her expectantly, but she wanted to clean up before she sat down.

Noticing her obvious discomfort, he said, "Why don't you wash off in the water while I get the food ready?"

She felt her face flame red. "I think I'm going to have to take off my pants to get all the mud off."

"Will it make you more comfortable if I promise to behave like a gentleman?"

"How about like a eunuch?" she asked flippantly.

A look of anguish flitted across his strong features. His normal expression so quickly returned that she wondered if she'd imagined his pained reaction.

"You got it," he said gruffly. Turning his back to her, he busied himself with the lunch.

She stepped nervously out of her now stiff jeans and left them on the grass. Gingerly she waded out until the cool water had covered her skimpy jungle-print undies and circled her waist. After she rinsed off her legs, she splashed water on her flushed face for good measure. Then, for a moment, she simply stood still and let the water move against her. The river was surprisingly warm. As it caressed her, she allowed herself to imagine it was Jack's hand touching her.

Eight

Jack turned from setting out the silverware. Wendy stood at the edge of the river like Venus on the half shell. The jeans she clutched barely hid her lean, shapely legs. Some water had dampened her blouse, outlining her breasts. My God, but she was beautiful.

She ran a slender hand through the wet ends of her auburn curls. "Can you toss me your shirt?"

Taking off his shirt, he went to hand it to her. He stopped a few feet away, forcing himself to breathe evenly. Up close, he could see the drops of water that clung to her smooth cheeks, flushed by the hot sun. His hands burned to touch the fullness of her breasts, to rub his thumbs over the nipples, which made dark circles against the whiteness of her blouse. . . .

But he couldn't. Not yet. First he had to tell her his secret. He didn't think he could wait much longer.

What would she say when he told her that he was a thirty-year-old virgin? What would she think? Probably that there was something very wrong with him. Was he ready to explain it all to her? Could he make her understand? What if she rejected him?

Looking into her soft brown eyes, he saw a sensual awareness that matched his—as well as what looked like uncertainty. Did she wonder why he wasn't touching her?

Against his will, his hand reached out to caress the soft skin of her neck. He told himself he just wanted to reassure her that she was beautiful and desirable, but really, he couldn't stop himself. When his hand met her sun-warmed skin, she started. Then she seemed to sway against him. Against his better judgment, he lowered his lips to brush against hers. They were sweet, warm. His tongue flicked out to lick away the drops of water that clung to her rosy mouth.

A soft sigh escaped—was it his or hers?

Her eyes were dark pools that threatened to engulf him. If he dove in, would he ever resurface? He'd resisted this pull so frequently in the past that it had become almost second nature to him. Reluctantly he withdrew his hand from the warmth of Wendy's neck. He let his hand drop to his side.

Doubt rekindled in her eyes. How he hated this! He had to explain his behavior, but first he had to wrestle with his own demons.

"Forgive me," he said.

"For what?"

"The kiss . . ." And everything else he hadn't done.

"Why? I enjoyed it."

How could she cut through his defenses so easily? "I did, too, but I can't do this. . . ."

Anger and hurt warred in her expression. "I don't understand." She closed her eyes, as if she were in pain. "But if that's what you want—"

"No," he said too loudly. "I don't *want* to stop." Hearing the harshness in his voice, he tried to control his frustration. "I don't know how to explain. . . ."

"Please," she said, folding her arms protectively across her chest. "If you're not attracted to me, you don't have to explain."

"That's not it. I just can't talk about it. . . ."

"Just forget it, okay?" she said quickly. "This is embarrassing. We stopped to have lunch. Let's do that. Now, can I have your shirt please?" She held out her hand.

He'd hurt her. That was the last thing he'd wanted to do. His stupid ignorance stopped him from knowing what to do. How to fix this.

As she pulled the shirt on and buttoned it, he couldn't help noticing how her breasts strained against the fabric. His shirt reached her knees, effectively covering her silky-looking thighs. How would it feel to trace his fingers along their sinuous length? When he looked down at his hands, they were quivering. What was it about her that sent his self-control careening over the edge like a car on a suicide run?

Before he gave in to temptation and touched her again, he made himself walk over to the picnic blanket and sit down. Today was turning out to be a miserable mistake. No doubt she thought he was a jerk, a sex-crazed fiend, or a major nerd.

"Here." He handed her a paper plate. "Have some potato salad." There, that was a sparkling opening line. Angry at himself, he turned to stare at the rippling water.

When he looked back, she was arranging a big cloth napkin over her bare legs for maximum coverage. He caught a glimpse of jungle-print underpants. Something hot and wild stirred inside him.

He took a spoonful of potato salad and swallowed quickly, nearly choking. A coughing spasm overtook him.

"Are you all right?" Her expression held concern mingled with amusement.

No, he wasn't okay. He'd lost his mind. She was driving him into a frenzy of sexual frustration. How could she sit there, half-naked, and ask if he was all right. "Just fine. Went down the wrong pipe."

"Have some soda." She handed him a can.

"Thanks."

"Sure." She seemed to be softening toward him again.

Good tactic to remember. After he behaved like a jerk, he'd just make a fool out of himself and disarm her. That shouldn't be too hard. He seemed to do that naturally around Wendy.

"We've got a turkey and roast beef sandwich," he said, deliberately making his tone friendly and unconcerned. "What would you like?"

"Roast beef."

Good choice. Leave the turkey, for the turkey. He handed her a sandwich, then unwrapped his. A soft wind blew through the giant firs that lined the banks of the river. Together they sat on the blanket, eating in something less than companionable silence.

After finishing her lunch, Wendy picked up her jeans. "I'm going to go clean these off."

"Okay," he said. "I'll pack up."

He kept an eye on her while he loaded the canoe. With childlike vigor, she slapped her jeans against a tree to knock off the dried mud. When she slipped into the pants and began pulling them up over her firm bottom, he had to look away.

Distraction. That's what he needed. Jogging across the small beach, he easily scaled a small hill that overlooked the dense forest stretching off into the distance. At the crest, he brought his breathing under control.

A crashing sound broke the stillness. Turning, Jack spotted a large brown bear. He froze. This wasn't the sort of distraction he'd had in mind. The animal rose up on its hind legs, its matted fur glinting dully in the sunlight. Then the bear dropped to the ground and began to lumber toward him.

Instinctively Jack took a step backwards. His foot hit a tree root, and suddenly he was tumbling sideways down a small ravine. Cursing, he tried to stop his fall, and felt a tendon give in his ankle. Up above, he heard the bear go crashing off through the woods. Jack's body came to a jarring stop against a tree.

"Ooof." Closing his eyes, he tried to blot out the throbbing pain in his ankle.

"Jack, where are you?" Wendy's voice sounded frantic.

"Down here," he said, gritting his teeth.

Scrambling over crumbling dirt and roots, Wendy followed his voice. She found Jack propped up against a tree trunk, his T-shirt muddied and ripped, and his face pale. "Are you all right?"

"Yeah, but I think I twisted my ankle."

"What happened?"

Shifting carefully, he looked as if he was in pain. "I saw a bear. . . ."

"A bear? Where?"

"Up at the top there. But he's gone now." He winced. "I scared him when I tripped."

She felt a smile tug the corners of her mouth. "You did make a God-awful lot of noise."

"Yeah. It's a special diversionary tactic I learned in Boy Scouts— scream like a banshee and fall down." A disgusted look on his face, he continued, "What a stupid thing to do!"

"Were you trying to protect me by scaring the bear away?"

"Are you nuts? I was running for my life." Normal color had returned to his face.

"Serves you right." Laughing, she sat down next to him on the dark, mossy ground.

The large fir at his back cast a shadow across his strong features. She wanted to reach out and touch his face, to kiss him until his mocking smile was replaced by a look of hunger.

Silence overtook them. No matter how much she liked him, she had to remember he was an unknown quantity, not a safe bet. He was tormented by something that he wouldn't share with her— something that kept getting in the way. What was it?

Hugging herself against the cool wind that blew through the trees, she noticed the shadows had lengthened. "It's getting late. Shouldn't we start back?"

"You're right. We'd better hustle or we'll be going against the tide." When he tried to stand, his face contorted with pain.

"Let me help you."

She stood next to him and braced his large frame. He smelled of pine needles, soap, and some indefinable male smell. Except for their kisses, they'd never been this close before. She reveled in the way he towered over her, like the redwoods in the forest, and how his firm muscles felt beneath her fingers. Get a grip, girl, she told herself.

"Are you sure you can walk?"

"Yep. I'll be fine."

He was not a man who revealed his feelings easily. While she liked his uncomplaining attitude, it made it harder to help him. Just like it made it harder to get close to him.

"Lean on me while we go uphill."

He shot her an amused look.

"Go on," she told him tartly. "I may be small, but I'm tough."

"Tell me about it." He leaned on her a little more. "You *are* strong," he admitted, his voice tinged with surprise.

Together they made their way up the hill, then she helped him into the canoe. He insisted on sitting in the front seat.

When she protested, he snapped, "I hurt my ankle, not my arms." After awkwardly tucking his long legs under him, he picked up his oars.

They pushed themselves away from the sandy beach and into the water. It was easy going the first half hour. Then the incoming tide hit them. Her arms began to ache. After what seemed like an eternity, she took her eyes off the hostile water and looked around.

"We passed that part of the shore five minutes ago," she said in dismay. "We're going backwards! This isn't going to work."

"We'll just have to paddle harder," he said, his breath coming in quick pants. "If we need to, I'll get out and pull us alongside the bank."

"Right. With a sprained ankle. And while you're at it, why don't you do a jig?"

"Don't give up or the tide will push us back up the river. We don't want to spend the night out here without sleeping bags or food."

Maybe she was wrong. Maybe they could make it back if they just kept paddling. Grumbling to herself, she rowed harder. She could see the muscles on Jack's back straining as he worked. After another fifteen minutes, her arms were throbbing.

"Jack. I've got to stop for a while."

"I'll keep paddling." An undercurrent of exhaustion laced his voice.

"Look at me."

When he turned, she saw beads of sweat on his white face. Panic seized her. He looked like he was going to pass out. What would she do with a sleeping giant in a canoe that was being pushed inexorably upstream?

"Okay, that's it," she said. "We're going to have to go back in the morning. We'll let the river take us back to the cabin we saw earlier. I'm sure we can stay there overnight. Or maybe the owner has a motorboat and can take us back."

She brightened at the idea. Maybe he had a pot of homemade beef stew and freshly baked bread to share with impromptu guests. Or a microwave and some Lean Cuisine. Even frozen food sounded delicious. All she wanted was warmth, food, and a wall between her and the dark, unpredictable forces of nature. Or was it Jack she needed to be separated from?

"Okay," he agreed. He must feel worse than she'd thought.

Fifteen minutes later they spotted the cabin. Finding a rope lying on the dock, she fastened their canoe securely. Jack limped to the cabin. Although one of the windows was open, no one answered when she knocked.

"I'll climb in," she said.

Before he could disagree, she pulled herself up on the ledge and scrambled through the window into a small, relatively clean kitchen. In one corner stood a wood-burning stove next to a free-standing basin. Hmm, no refrigerator, no lights, no electricity. At least the cabin had a roof. And walls. It would do.

Wendy heard Jack knocking on the front door. "Open up!"

When she let him in, he hobbled over to the couch in the tiny living room and collapsed into its frayed pillows. "Ah. That feels great." Curiously he looked around. "Not bad."

"A bit rustic, though." She sighed. "There go my fantasies of a warm, home-cooked meal and a friendly host with a motorboat to take us back to civilization."

"Yep. Looks like we're on our own tonight."

A surge of anxiety ran through her body, followed by excitement. To hide her nervousness, she went to stand next to the massive fireplace that dominated the living area. A pile of logs flanked the hearth made of river rock. Two miner's lamps stood on the wooden mantel, overshadowed by a deer's head, which stared imperiously out at the room.

"I guess we'll really get to rough it tonight," she said.

"Hardly. We're on easy street. We have a roof over our heads, a fireplace, and a . . . ." He looked around the compact room. The cabin seemed to hold only the living room, a small nook with a table, and the kitchen. "No bedroom, huh?"

When he stood as if to explore, he gritted his teeth.

Forestalling him, she stepped in front of him. "Sit, let me look. Maybe this is the bedroom. . . ." She opened a door. A heavy coat, a rifle, fishing gear, and several of the ugliest hats she'd ever seen stared back at her. "Nope. Unless we want to sleep standing upright."

"I'll pass." He pointed to a neatly rolled pile of blankets in the corner. "This must be what our mystery host uses as a bed."

One bedroll, two people. The images that unrolled in her mind made her suddenly nervous.

He shrugged his wide shoulders. "At least there's food. . . ." A look of doubt crossed his features. "Isn't there?"

"I hope so."

Going into the kitchen, she surveyed the contents of the cupboards. Leaning through the doorway, she asked him, "It depends. Do you consider Boston baked beans, Vienna sausages, and packaged macaroni and cheese food?"

"Close enough. Wait, let me help—" he began.

"It's too early for dinner," she said, not wanting him to put pressure on his sprained ankle. Going back to the living room, she sat in an armchair. "Why don't you relax?"

"Okay," he said reluctantly. "Thanks."

His foot looked suspiciously swollen. She wanted to take off his sock, massage his ankle, bring him hot compresses. . . . Hold it. With the strange undercurrents between them, she'd be safest doing nothing that could be misinterpreted.

There wasn't anything to do but to sit in the living room, facing each other, until the sun set and it was time to go to bed. Wherever that might be. Or mean. The cabin started to seem claustrophobic. She had to get out.

"I'm going to go look around outside. Put your feet up on the sofa while I'm gone. Can I get you anything before I leave?" Who was she trying to be, the Miss Manners of the Wilderness?

"Like a can of Boston beans?" He stretched his long legs out on the sofa. "No, thanks. I'm fine. Be careful. There might be bears around here, too."

She went out the back door onto a wooden veranda, then down

the stairs that led to a lovely glen. Following a well-worn path in the grass, she entered the woods. Staying within sight of the cabin, she gathered blackberries, mint leaves, and some nasturtiums.

When she returned half an hour later, she found Jack on the sofa, fast asleep. For a moment she just watched him. His eyelashes lay in a dark crescent against his tanned skin. The dangerous, barely restrained quality he normally had was softened, making him look vulnerable and boyish.

Quietly she went into the kitchen. Opening a few cans, she put the contents on some plates. When she brought them into the living room, Jack was sitting up, his blue eyes bright and his normal intensity restored.

"I needed that catnap." He looked down at the motley assortment of cold food on the plate she handed him. "Vienna sausages, beans, blackberries, and . . . flowers?"

"They're supposed to be edible," she said, plopping down on a pillow at the foot of an armchair. The colorful arrangement on the plates pleased her.

He bit off the head of a fiery red nasturtium, chewed it, then made a face. "I always knew you Californians were wacky, but this is going too far."

"We Californians? Where are you from, O superior one?"

"Maine."

She pondered that answer. "That makes sense."

"How so?"

"You're too driven to be a mellow California *dude*."

She seemed to have struck a chord. His open expression closed down in a way that had become familiar to her. What was he hiding?

"I'm about as far removed from a 'laid-back dude' as one can get."

"How'd you end up in California?"

"Came here to go to school."

"Oh, really? Where?"

"A place you wouldn't know in Menlo Park."

Somehow she suspected that she'd trespassed into another area that was off limits for unknown reasons. Outside the cabin, the sun was setting, darkening the living room until they were sitting in near shadows. A cold wind started to blow, seeping in through the cracks in the old cabin.

"Time to start a fire," he said, standing gingerly.

"Should you walk on your foot?"

"It feels much better, thanks." Kneeling, he began to pile logs in the fireplace, the curve of his muscular back outlined in the half-light.

He got the kindling going. After a few minutes, a small fire began to lick the edges of the logs. Next he lit the two miner's lamps on the mantel. A soft glow filled the living room, transforming it into a cozy, rustic world.

Unwrapping a warm quilt from the bedroll, he draped it over her shoulders. "Here. This will take the edge off the chill." His hands lingered for a moment longer than necessary.

Her senses stirred at the intimate gesture. "Thanks."

Taking a blanket for himself, he sat down on the sofa. The firelight flickered over his handsome, strong features. She tried not to stare, but the mix of strength, pain, and sensitivity in his face drew her eyes back again and again.

Turning, he intercepted her glance. "Come sit by me," he said, holding out his hand. "It's closer to the fire."

She did—making sure to keep to her corner of the sofa. After all, she just wanted to get warm. As attractive as he was, she'd be crazy to get involved with this enigmatic man. So that meant no touching. Not even playing footsie. She had to stay rational.

When he put part of his blanket over her legs, his hands brushed against her foot. Her eyes flew to his face.

Nine

His hand lingered on her foot, gently massaging it.

Warmth leapt from his fingers, like the flame engulfing the logs in the fireplace. Wendy looked into his deep blue eyes and saw another kind of light smoldering there.

He asked, "Are you warm enough?"

"I'm still a little chilled." Ice-cold with trepidation was a more honest description.

"Come here."

She took the hand he offered, feeling his strength, doubting her sanity. After he pulled her next to him on the sofa, he draped one arm over her shoulders in an easy, brotherly gesture that was anything but fraternal. The solid muscles of his leg pressed against her thigh.

She noted with curious detachment the softening that began in her limbs and continued in her heart. It felt so right to be curled up next to him that she couldn't pull herself away. Not yet.

Together they regarded the fire's seduction of the log. In the darkening cabin, the tiny fingers of flame made inroads against the seemingly impervious wood.

His touch was such a flame, burning up her resistance. She started to tremble.

Pulling her closer, he asked, "What is it?"

"Just tense, I guess."

"It's been a long day. You've been a good sport. This didn't turn out the way I'd planned."

"Me either."

His fingers traced the column of her throat. "How about a neck massage?"

Uh-oh, this way lay danger. But who could be sane in the face of such a warm glance, such an eager touch? "Sounds wonderful."

He began to rub his thumbs along the tendons in the back of her neck—his caresses sure, hot, and as insistent as the fire coiling around the wood. Relaxing, she let the tension leave her tired muscles.

"It's strange not to have TV or radio," she ventured. "Just the fire. Makes me wonder how people entertained themselves before they had electricity."

"Maybe they did this." His husky voice tickled her skin, making the fine hairs stand up on the back of her neck. Trailing his fingers down, he kneaded the muscles in her upper back.

He could be right. No wonder families had been much larger then. When someone touched you like this, it was easy to forget anything but the impulse to touch back. . . . She had to stay sensible, she reminded herself.

His fingers continued their sensual exploration up onto her shoulders. She leaned back against his broad chest. So much for sense and sensibility.

"Umm," she murmured. "That feels great."

"You're a bundle of nerves. You needed this massage. It's a tough job . . ."

"But someone had to do it."

His chuckle ruffled her hair. "Lucky me."

As his hands moved in ever larger circles across her chest, they grazed the tops of her breasts. Her breath caught in her throat.

Suddenly his hands stilled. "We have to talk."

Jeez, the man had the worst timing in the world! He'd invited her to enter a nonverbal world of sensation. She'd agreed. What was his problem now? Turning, she scanned his face. She had thought she'd wanted honesty, but what she saw there made her afraid. What terrible secret was he going to reveal?

She frowned. "You're married, aren't you?"

His laugh burst out of him. "Hardly."

Hardly. She didn't like the sound of that one bit. Did that mean only married a little bit—like on weekends? Or did it mean he was recently separated, divorced, or perhaps a twentieth-century Bluebeard? With his face bronzed by the glow of the fireplace, he looked honorable, above reproach—but they say mass murderers can look just like the rest of us.

"What, then? Are you a criminal?"

He shook his head. "Remember I said I came out here to go to school?"

"Yes." Anxiety always made her want to tell jokes. Usually bad ones. Clutching her chest, she said in a weak voice, "Don't tell me. . . . You're not a"—gasp—"college dropout, are you?"

"Sorry, I graduated with honors." He paused, then continued, "I came out here to go to a special sort of school."

"What kind of special school?" How long could he string this out? The man was driving her crazy.

"Seminary school."

She gave him a blank look. "Seminary school?" What? This vital, sexy man wearing black jackets with a white collar, saying mass and . . . No, it was too hard to believe. He couldn't be a priest.

She swallowed. "You mean you're a minister?"

"No, no. I was studying to be a priest. Until two years ago, when I dropped out."

"Why?"

"I realized I couldn't make a commitment to God in that way. I still want to help people. . . ."

"And you do," she said slowly, starting to piece the puzzle together, "at the shelter."

"Right." He stretched as if he'd been released from a confined space. "Boy, that's a weight off my chest."

"I'm still confused. If you're not a priest, why can't you touch me?" She sat bolt upright on the sofa and stared into his impossibly beautiful eyes. "You aren't gay, are you?"

"No, I'm not."

At least she hadn't completely lost her mind. "What does this mean, then?"

"I'm, well, inexperienced."

"Oh, is that all?" She snuggled against him. "That's perfectly natural since you were studying to be a priest. You know, I've had a couple of boyfriends, but I'm no Mata Hari myself."

He gently extricated himself from her arms, then hobbled over to stand before the fire. "No, I'm *really* inexperienced."

"Okay, but it's only been two years."

"I don't think you understand." He stared into the raging fire. "I'm a virgin."

"A what?"

"A virgin." He shot her a sardonic grin. "You know, the creature Madonna sings about. A virgin. A thirty-year-old virgin."

She saw the pain in his eyes that he'd tried to keep out of his voice. It went straight through her heart. What a difficult thing for a man of his pride and age to admit. She wanted to comfort him, but the last thing he needed was to be treated like a child.

No wonder he'd behaved in such baffling ways. She mulled the notion over in her mind. Was he telling her because he wanted her to help him fix the problem? Or was he warning her away?

She forced herself to ask, "Do you want to, um, change that?"

"More than you can know." His dark eyes met hers.

"Oh." A delicious melting started inside her.

"How do you feel about me being a virgin?"

How did she feel?

Flattered. There was something very special about the thought of being his first love.

Concerned. She wanted to make his first experience special.

Excited. It would be fun to show him the ropes, as it were.

A rush of emotion overwhelmed her, making tears sting her eyes. He was such a strong man. Such a tender man.

"I think it's exciting." She went to stand next to him by the fire, taking his large, well-shaped hand in hers. "You know," she said softly, "I never would've guessed. You're so naturally sexy."

He searched her eyes, as if testing her sincerity. "I thought my inexperience was painfully obvious."

"It wasn't. I'd just about decided that you weren't attracted to me."

"Don't ever think that." He pulled her tightly against him. "You're beautiful. I've had the devil's time keeping my hands to myself."

"Then it's time to stop holding yourself back."

"Ah!" His words broke from his lips in a tight cry. "You don't know what you do to me."

Lowering his lips, he took her mouth in a kiss of frustration and desire. He slowly began to rub his body against hers. She could feel his erection. Knowing she excited him made her heart beat faster.

"Let's get comfortable," he said.

"Good idea." She took his hand as they walked to the sofa.

"Wait here," he said.

She heard some rustling in the cupboards, then he limped back with clean sheets.

"Before my catnap, I did a little exploring." He laid the sheets on the floor in front of the fire.

From her comfortable spot on the sofa, she watched him make a bed with the blankets from the bedroll. "For someone who's new at this, you sure seem to know what you're doing."

Backlit by the flames, he stood and faced her.

"I know what I want. I just never allowed myself to go after it before." His eyes met hers. "Besides, I've imagined this a thousand times since I met you."

A frisson of delicious anticipation moved down her spine. Experienced or inexperienced, this man did something wonderful to her insides.

Taking his open hand, she let him pull her to her feet. He began to unbutton her blouse. She could see the concentration in his expression. His hands shook the tiniest bit. When one button caught, he tried unsuccessfully to untangle it.

"Damn!"

"Relax." Taking his hands, she gently put them at his sides. "Let me undress you."

Slowly she began to undo his shirt, stopping every few seconds to plant kisses on the warm skin of his chest. She'd dreamt about *this* several times herself. When she slipped his shirt off his shoulders, the flickering firelight outlined his body. He looked like a Greek statue: well-defined muscles cloaked in smooth skin.

She started to unbutton her own blouse. His hungry eyes watched every move. When she reached the last button, he put his hands on the collar of her blouse.

"My turn."

He eased off her blouse, revealing her white lacy bra. He tried to unsnap the front of the skimpy garment, frustration building in his face.

"Wait," she said, "let me help. . . ."

"I can do it. It's only a bra, not a straitjacket."

"But—"

"I've almost got it." He tugged harder.

"Yes, but I want to wear it again," she said, unhooking it. "It fastens in the back."

"Ah! My next guess."

"I suspected as much." She let the slip of fabric dangle before dropping it to the floor.

For a moment, he simply stared. When he let a shaky breath out, she thought her heart would burst. Then he cupped her firm breasts, letting their soft weight rest in his hands. He measured her breasts with wonder, touching her as if he never thought he would get the chance. His thumbs traced the outlines of her nipples—tentatively at first, then with growing urgency.

"You're so soft," he said, his voice low and filled with a frightening intensity, "Do you realize how beautiful you are?"

Unable to bring herself to speak, she smiled instead.

He ran his hands down the skin of her sides, then slid his fingers inside the waist of her jeans. His hands were warm against her hipbones. After unsnapping her jeans, he slipped them off her legs. She stood before him in her jungle-print underwear and nothing else. Suddenly shy, she felt almost as if *she* were the virgin. Self-consciously she covered her breasts with her arms.

"No, let me look at you." With aching tenderness, he opened her arms, then ran his hands along her hips, belly, and up to her breasts. "I've dreamed about this moment." His hands stopped. "I don't mean to be indelicate, but are you protected?"

"Yes." How thoughtful of him!

When she reached out to trace the sensual shape of his lips, he took her finger into his mouth and gently nipped it.

"And this?" he asked. "Do you feel comfortable about all this?"

"Shhh." She breathed her words against the inviting line of his neck. "First lesson: No more talking."

"Okay, teach." His white teeth flashed.

She unzipped his jeans. With his help, she slipped them off his strong, lean legs. Dressed in nothing but their underwear, they faced each other. He quickly pulled off his briefs, then hooked his thumbs under the wisp of silk that embraced her hips. For a moment, his hands lingered on her hipbones.

"You're the only woman I know who could wear jungle-print underwear and pull it off."

"Me pull it off? I thought that was *your* job."

"Something this fun can't be called a job."

With tantalizing slowness, he slipped her panties off her legs. She felt hot color tinge her cheeks at the ardent look in his eyes. She tried to remember exactly how she had felt as a virgin—the mix of anticipation laced with fear. Watching the emotions flit across his face was like having her first time again.

"You're magnificent," he said, his voice deep and dark like the night outside. "Your body just calls out to be touched."

"You're not so bad yourself, partner." She trailed her hands over the springy hair on his thighs.

Despite the light tone of their banter, she felt tension building inside her. How long could she stand this slow torture, this exchange of touches that was like honey dripping and pooling on a sultry day? Suddenly he pulled her down alongside him on the bear rug. The man learned fast!

Beside her, the fire crackled, sending light and warmth over them. When Jack reached for her, his callused fingertips generated a different heat in her skin.

"Let me touch you for a while," he said.

He reverently caressed her breasts and stroked the skin of her belly and thighs as if he'd never held a naked woman in his arms. Then she remembered—he hadn't. She stretched and turned like a flower unfolding before the sun. There was something to be said for his inexperience, she thought. He held her as if she were a Ming vase: delicate, one of a kind, and infinitely precious.

"I could do this all night," he said.

"Umm. Normally I wouldn't complain, but there are so many other things we could do, too."

"Haste makes waste," he drawled as his fingertips teased her nipples, sending shivers up the length of her body.

"True." She nibbled on his ear. "But to everything there is a season, isn't that so?"

"True."

She took his hand and placed it between her legs. "Touch me here."

Feeling a little embarrassed at her own boldness, she raised her eyes to meet his. He searched her face, his eyes almost obsidian in the firelight. He seemed surprised at her directness. She was, too. But something about his combination of innocence and mastery made her daring.

At first his fingers moved carefully, almost awkwardly. As she shifted in response and became slick, he touched her with growing certainty. He found a rhythm that teased and goaded her, sending sensations coursing through her body. Stronger, then softer, then stronger again.

"That's wonderful," she whispered.

"I think so, too."

She looked up to see a smile illuminate his features.

Running her hands up his legs, she reveled in the feel of warm skin over muscles. She let her hands flutter to his chest, circle his beaded nipples, and skim over his quickly rising ribs.

"You're driving me crazy." His features were strained as if he was on the edge of losing control. "Touch *me* now." Capturing her hand, he moved it to the nest of dark hair between his legs.

She clasped her hand around him, feeling him surge against her fingers. A sigh escaped him, quickly followed by one from her.

"Ah, yes." His voice had a strangled sound. "Very nice."

"Are you all right?"

"Is being insanely happy 'all right'?"

"I'd say."

She pressed a kiss on his forehead, his cheekbones, his mouth. He returned the pressure of her lips, sliding his tongue into her mouth. The tight mood slipped away, subsumed in the fixed intensity of his touch. The deepening kiss kept pace with the movement of his fingers. His breath coming faster, he used his hand to urge her legs apart. With surprising gentleness, he rolled on top of her, supporting his weight on his hands.

"Am I crushing you?"

"No." She was amazed at his control. And his concern.

When he pressed against her, she used her hand to guide him. With a thrust, he entered her. She gasped. It felt so right to be with him like this. She felt filled up, fused with him.

He hesitated, as if he were enjoying the sensation of being enveloped. Raising her eyes, she saw a look almost of pain cross his face. Why was he feeling that now? Was he disappointed? The thought hurt her more than she would have expected.

"You feel so good," he said, dispelling her doubts.

"Don't stop." She tilted her pelvis, encouraging him to move. The tension inside her urged her to get close to him, as close as she could.

Together they began to find the tempo of the oldest dance. Just as she started to unfurl like a bud in blossom, he sped up. *No, no,* she wanted to call out, but she stopped herself. Quickly, too quickly, he stiffened and let out a cry, then collapsed against her.

This was the downside of his inexperience. She didn't want to bum his high, but he'd finished a bit too quickly.

After a moment, he rolled on his side, regarding her with unnerving intensity. She struggled to look neutral.

"I'm sorry," he said. "That was too fast, wasn't it?"

Baby steps, she reminded herself. We all learn in baby steps. "No, I'm just, uh, basking in the afterglow."

"You're a terrible liar."

Staring into his eyes, she saw his vulnerability and strength. If the tables were turned, would she have his courage? The very least she owed him was the truth.

"Okay, the beginning was wonderful. You made me feel so special." Leaning over, she kissed him. "It's just that . . . well, it was a little fast at the end there."

"I was afraid of that. I tried to slow down, but it was too incredible. I hope I didn't disappoint you, but, well . . . your look sort of tells it all."

"Wait, I'm not trying to make you feel bad. You asked and . . ." Damn, she'd put her whole leg in her mouth this time.

He lovingly brushed a strand of hair off her forehead. "The truth isn't going to kill me."

She relaxed. "I am afraid you'd be crushed."

"Crushed? Are you kidding? I just have to keep doing it until I get it right."

She couldn't stop herself from chuckling at his lusty grin.

He nuzzled the soft skin of her breasts, then placed love bites along the curve of her shoulder. He asked, "So what do we do to make it last longer?"

"Lots of practice."

He drew his index finger down her nose and around her lips. "Once a day?"

She nipped the tip of his finger.. "At the bare minimum."

"Several times a day?"

"That would be best. In the beginning, at least."

"I see." The stubble on his chin tickled the column of her throat. "Can I count on your help?"

"Absolutely." She met his glance, then his lips. "Let's get started, shall we?" Her hand trailed across the sleek skin of his back, shaping the firm muscles of his derriere.

As he pulled her on top of him, he whispered, "You taskmaster, you."

Ten

When Jack awoke, moonlight was streaming in through the window in the cabin's living room. It had to be around midnight. Reaching out, he felt Wendy's warm, naked body. Desire hit him again. With knockout force. He had thought he'd have to wait, but his body said now was just fine. Turning, he looked at her. She was staring up at the ceiling, a contented half smile on her face.

Inside he felt a twinge of anxiety. She had opened herself up to him—offered not just her body but herself. That meant he had the power to hurt her. Did he really want that responsibility? He had thought so, but suddenly he wasn't so sure.

A part of him wanted time to be selfish, to explore this newfound thrill—without having to worry about her needs, her desires. He felt disgusted with himself. That sounded selfish, shallow, wrong.

In the past, he'd always known exactly where he stood—with himself, with others, with God. Now he wasn't certain about anything. Especially himself.

Jack looked up to meet her gaze. Rolling on her side, she propped her head on one hand. Her shoulders and rounded breasts gleamed in the moonlight.

"You're so quiet," she said. "Can I assume that the experience was so earth-shattering, you've forgotten how to talk?"

He couldn't help but laugh. "Something like that."

She looked more closely at him. "Sure you're okay?"

"Yeah." He swallowed. "And you?"

"I was until I saw that look of terror on your face."

He felt himself relax a little. Thank the Lord she still had her sense of humor. "This is all new for me. I'd hate to make a mistake."

"You're doing great so far."

"Thanks." He tried to silence his inner doubts. He'd lost his virginity—expecting everything to be easier afterwards. Guess it wasn't that simple. His body's inexperience wasn't the problem. It was his mind.

But anyone in his situation would be disconcerted. He'd figure it out. Wouldn't he?

"Jack? What is it?"

Her voice penetrated the sticky web of his thoughts. A fierce desire to protect her streaked through him. To protect her from himself and who he might turn out to be.

"Thinking too much," he said gruffly "It's a problem I have."

"Don't think. Just be here with me. Now."

It sounded so easy, so tempting. He'd simply have to prove to her—and himself—that he could learn how to handle this new kind of relationship.

"Okay, let's start over," he said. "Hi, gorgeous."

"Hi, yourself."

Curling a hand around the nape of her neck, he threaded his fingers in her soft hair. He loved being able to touch her like this—without feeling that he was doing something wrong or forbidden.

"Mmm," she said, her voice husky. "I like a man who takes his studies seriously."

"You did say practice makes perfect."

The first time they'd made love had been fast, furious, and—for him, at least—fantastic. But now he planned to slow down and savor each moment. He'd start by looking, not touching. She lay on the bear rug, her small body lithe and sweetly curved. His glance traveled from her face, down her neck to the creamy skin of her breasts, across her belly and downward to the triangle of curls at the top of her legs.

Okay, that was enough restraint. A man could only stand so much.

He'd begin by experimenting with touch—to try and figure out what felt good to her. Reaching out, he tilted up her chin so he could see her face more clearly in the moonlight. Pink blossomed under her tan cheeks. Was she feeling shy? How unexpected. And charming.

Gently, he touched her high cheekbones. The taut skin there was smooth, unblemished. With a forefinger he traced the delicate arch of her brows. She was lovely, almost exotic-looking with her dark curls and café au lait complexion. Her brown eyes—velvety, mysterious—watched his every move. Eyes a man could drown in.

The last thing he wanted was to seem like an over-eager seventeen-year-old, but he couldn't hide his enthusiasm if he tried. Reaching out, he cupped her firm breasts. Did she see that his hands shook?

"These are incredible!" As soon as he said it, he realized how impersonal it sounded. "I mean, your breasts are beautiful. What an invention."

She chuckled. "I'm flattered."

He held and tested their weight, amazed at the way her dusky nipples pulled together into tight nubs at his touch. What a marvelous thing the female form was! And hers in particular.

Doubt brought him up short. Last night he'd been the fastest gun in the West, and now he was going as slow as the proverbial turtle. He looked up at her. "My timing's off again, isn't it?"

"Are you kidding? I like a man with a slow touch."

Taking her at her word, he let himself give in to his sense of awe. Was this a sweet dream or for real? To have the unfettered chance to explore, to touch, and to feel seemed too good to be true.

He moved his hands down to her waist. In the dimly lit room, her body gleamed softly, like polished silk. Incredible! And the texture of her skin was different from his. Her flesh was smoother, sleeker, more supple somehow. When she ran her nails down his inner thighs, he caught his breath. His skin might be coarser, but it worked just fine, thank you. Responded to touch. To the warmth of her fingers. To the slow pull of her nails across his belly. No doubt about it.

She shifted, and he caught a whiff of her scent—sweet, light, some sort of flower. Orange blossom maybe. He smoothed his hand along the curve of one thigh, marveling at her combination of sleek flesh and firm muscle.

Smiling at him, she let out a shaky sigh. Her brown eyes were wide open, her soft lips quivering. "A woman could get used to all this attention."

"I could spend all day doing this."

"You'll get no complaints from me."

He dragged his hands down the taut line of her belly to the soft nest of curls at the top of her legs. She moaned. He liked the sound. And, regardless of his doubts, this learning process was certain to be fun.

"I want to touch you, too," she said.

He pressed his lips against her warm mouth. "Not now."

"But—"

"But nothing. It's part of my training." He pinned her arms above her head, watching the way her breasts lifted. God, she was beautiful. "Besides, it's your turn."

He wanted to make her feel the way she had made him feel: connected, on fire. Wanted her to twist and turn with the same heat that raged through his body, hardening him, driving him, until he could barely control himself.

He started by kissing every perfect inch of her, from her forehead down to the soft skin on the arch of her feet. When she tried to respond, he wouldn't let her.

"Hold still," he said.

"I can't take much more of this," she gasped.

"Don't like it?"

"I love it."

White heat surged through him. A mix of power and joy. He slipped a hand between her legs. Wet and hot, incredible. Her body began to writhe, her breath grew ragged. He rubbed his fingers back and forth, loving the feel of her. With his tongue, he traced her collarbone, the edge of one breast, then circled the nipple. She arched her back, pressing herself against his lips. Following her cues, he sucked a dusky rose tip into his mouth and bit gently.

"That's not bad either." Her voice was strangled.

Inside him, the fire kept building, getting hotter and hotter. He was torn between wanting to rush forward and wanting to delay the pleasure. He forced himself to think of the stock market, the rowdiest kid at the shelter, anything but how great she felt.

"Please," she said, her voice breathless and urgent. "I want you inside me now."

Pushing open her legs, he pressed his erection against her, then stopped. He waited for her signal. When she tilted her pelvis up, he couldn't hold himself back anymore. Plunging inside, he sheathed himself in her warmth. A moan escaped from deep in his chest. He had always suspected he had a passionate nature, but he'd had no idea how strong that part of him was. Or how much that sexual self had craved expression.

Slowly he pulled back, then pressed into her again. With sure, deliberate strokes, he began to make love to her.

Whatever doubts he had, he would face them later. Right now he gave himself permission to enjoy this still new experience which he'd fantasized about a thousand times over.

She met every move of his with a thrust of her own. Finally her body arched up, then she cried out. He felt a moment of satisfaction that he'd pleased her. Then his self-control began to give way. His body took on a rhythm of its own. He thrust faster and faster, until he went rocketing over the edge, exploding into a fireball. Collapsing against her, he buried his face in her neck.

"You just made the honor roll." She sounded stunned.

"I had a good teacher."

He cradled her body against his chest, tangling his legs with hers. She was so sweet, so very sweet. Before sleep crashed down, his last thought was that he'd only put his demons at arm's length—and they'd be back in full force later.

As the sun crept over the treetops and into the cabin, Jack trailed kisses from Wendy's breasts to her neck. For once in her life, she welcomed dawn. Never mind coffee. He'd do just fine as a wake-up call. Heck, if every morning began this way, she could become addicted to the first light of day.

"You were fantastic last night," he said. "I can't believe I missed out on such a wonderful part of life for so long."

"Truly a waste." She threw off the blankets and let her body do what it wanted to do—press itself along the firm length of his thighs and torso. "Especially when you're such a natural at all . . . this."

" 'All this'?" His tone was teasing.

"Making love. Getting close. Doing the antler dance."

"The 'antler dance'?" He pulled her to her feet.

"You know what I mean."

"Mmmm." He kicked the bedroll out of the way. Pulling her naked body against his, he began to turn in slow circles in front of the fireplace.

"What are you doing?"

"What are *we* doing, you mean." Rubbing his chin on the top of her head, he whispered, "Umm. You smell good."

"You didn't answer my question." She smiled up at him.

"I'm waltzing with you."

Noticing his limp, she tried to stop him. "You'll hurt your ankle again!"

"Relax. This is my moment to celebrate. Share it with me, would you?" He twirled her around again.

His enthusiasm was infectious. She relaxed into his strong hold and the spontaneous joy of their dance. She was relieved. Last night she'd been worried, uncertain about what his sudden silences had meant. But his mood seemed lighter today. Outside the birds sang, and the trees swayed in the morning breeze. A moment of happiness moved through her like a wave of sweet water.

"You know, this is ridiculous," she said.

"Hey, a woman who calls making love 'the antler dance' shouldn't be telling anyone else what's ridiculous."

"You may have a point there."

"It's fun, isn't it?" His body was hardening against hers.

"Deliciously so," she admitted.

"Let's move on to act two."

With those words, he pulled her down to the rug again. The last thing she saw before he lowered his head to kiss her was the stern face of the stag mounted above the fireplace, antlers gleaming in the morning sun. He was probably just jealous.

Back at Valencia House on Monday, Jack found himself humming out loud at odd moments. He tried to keep the smile off his face, but at the least provocation, he drifted off into fantasies about Wendy.

He had no idea what he was going to do in the long run—or even if he was capable of sustaining a romantic relationship. But for now, he gave up trying to control his errant mind. It had twenty years of catching up to do.

Mrs. Hughes shot him a calculating look. "Nice weekend?"

"Yes." Stupendous would be a better description. "Mendocino will be perfect for the kids." It certainly had been great for him. God, but Wendy had looked beautiful—all rosy and softly mussed—the morning after they'd first made love.

"I'll make the arrangements for the kids' camping trip." Cocking her head, she asked, "What do you need?"

Just Wendy in my bed on a daily basis ought to do it, Mrs. Hughes. "I'll make a list." That smile crept up on his face again. He tried to wipe it off. Mrs. Hughes didn't look fooled.

"Nice to see you so happy," she said innocently.

"Hmmm." Now he understood why Shakespeare wrote love poems. The desire to wax rhapsodical was strong.

As soon as Mrs. Hughes closed the door behind her, he picked up the phone and dialed Wendy's number.

She answered on the third ring. "Hello?"

"It's me."

"Jack." Her voice softened. "How nice to hear from you. It's been an hour since your last call. I was beginning to think you'd forgotten me." He could hear amusement and tenderness in her voice.

"Keeping track, huh?"

"I put a notch in one of my chairs every time you call. Pretty soon there won't be much left to sit on."

Jeez, had it only been an hour ago? He was losing all sense of time. Was he being too eager? Maybe it was time to pull back a little, be cool. Tap in to his rational self again. "I've been acting like a teenager with overactive hormones, huh?"

"Don't stop."

He felt another twinge. Lavishing all this attention on her when he had doubts—serious doubts—probably wasn't the smartest thing to do. Or the most honest, for that matter. He shook off his anxiety. For once in his life, he was going to act without thinking forever first. "Did you get my flowers?"

"You mean that floral arrangement in the shape of a bear was from you?"

"Who else?"

"The card confused me," she said. "I don't know a 'Dr. Love.' "

"Correction. You *didn't* know one."

"Okay, Doc. Do you make house calls?"

"Luckily for you, I'm one of the few remaining physicians who does."

"How soon can you get over here?" she asked.

He looked at his watch. "How about noon?"

"Sounds great." She lowered her voice to a whisper. "Nathan's gone for the afternoon."

"Even better. See you then."

The phone clicked. Putting his feet up on his desk, Jack winced at his sore ankle, then started to compose a love poem. Watch out, Shakespeare. Rereading his first few lines a while later, he decided the Bard was safe, but perhaps he could give the greeting card poets a run for their money.

Wendy had just thrown a pile of dirty clothes in the hall closet and tossed paint supplies on the bookshelf when Jack arrived. He greeted her with a lingering kiss. Then he pulled a crumpled paper out of his pocket and proudly handed it to her.

"What's this?" she asked.

"Read it."

She quickly scanned the poem, laughter welling up inside her.

It was terrible. Her glance flew to his face. Thank God he wasn't serious. "Oh, you shouldn't have." She batted her eyelashes at him.

"My pleasure."

"No, I'm serious." She waited a beat. "You really *shouldn't* have."

"That bad?"

"Let me put it to you gently: Don't quit your day job."

Snatching the paper away from her, he clutched it behind his back. "I'm deeply wounded that you don't like my poetry."

She kissed him, loving the way his warm lips felt. "I like it about as much as you like my furniture." She slipped her arms around him.

"Woman, you play hardball."

"I'm flattered you made the effort, but come on!" Grabbing the paper out of his hands, she leaped out of his reach.

She read out loud, " 'Roses are red, bears love honey. Even with a limp, Dr. Love'll give you a run for your money.' Or 'Wendy, Wendy, eyes of brown. In just one weekend, you turned my life upside down.' "

She let out a yelp as he grabbed her arm. Cornering her, he wrapped her in a big hug so she couldn't move. "You're too harsh on a rank beginner. The poem has a certain *je ne sais quoi.*"

"I don't know what it is either," she said, her eyes challenging him. "I just know it stinks."

"Them's fighting words."

With karate-like quickness, he swooped her up and carried her to the sofa. Together they tumbled on the couch, his body bracing her fall. After rolling on top of her, he tugged her blouse out of her jeans. Then his hands slipped under her top and began to caress her skin.

"This is fighting?" She lay beneath him, melting as his hands slowly inched up toward her breasts.

"First you disarm your enemy." As he unbuttoned her blouse, he pressed his lips on the quivering plane of her belly. "Make 'em think you're on their side."

"It's working," she gasped when his mouth surrounded one of her nipples.

"Surrender?"

"What are my options?"

"Give up or I'll seduce you into submission."

"I'll take door number two, Monty." A shudder moved through her body at the dark glint in his eyes.

What had she unleashed when she helped him lose his virginity? She began to unbutton his shirt. Did she dare believe that they were falling in love? Her hand stilled.

A sliver of doubt lodged itself in her mind. What if Jack wasn't falling in love, but was just infatuated with this new process?

Before her thoughts could travel any further down that disturbing path, he said, "Earth to Wendy."

"Sorry. I was thinking about something."

"Is my technique *that* bad?" He spoke in jest, but she could see a real question in his eyes.

"No, no." She felt a jolt of remorse that she wasn't telling him the complete truth about her reservations. Deep-sixing her guilt, she took his face in her hands and kissed him. "I've just been distracted lately. I've still got a lot of work to do for my upcoming art show." She nibbled at the edge of his mouth. "You're wonderful. Now, weren't you trying to neutralize me or something?"

The hurt look began to leave his eyes. "Or something."

"I'm yours."

She would have plenty of time to think later. His hand slid up her inner thigh.

Now was the time to feel.

After they resurfaced, Jack watched Wendy take a man's shirt from the closet and shrug it on with throwaway grace. Tearing his eyes from her slender body, he dressed. He'd had no idea what a sexual connection to a woman could do to his normally logical, rational mind. It put him on edge, out of synch with the self he used to know.

At the door, he pulled her against him. He looked first at her flushed face and then down at the shirt, which showed a glimpse of her shapely breasts. Possessiveness rushed through him, surprising him with its strength. "Is that an old boyfriend's?"

"No," she said. "It's mine. I have several."

"Why men's shirts?"

"When I was little, my dad traveled a lot. He was in the foreign service for Spain for several years, so he—"

He interrupted. "You never told me your dad was in the diplomatic corps." No wonder she was so sophisticated in certain ways. "What was that like?"

"Mostly it was a drag."

She had hardly talked about her family, so he followed her lead. "Why?"

"He was gone a lot. And when he was around, he was preoccupied. Too busy to have much time for a child."

"And the men's shirts?" he prompted when he saw a bleak look fill her eyes.

"One night when I was about three, I was crying because my dad had to go away. Again." Wrapping her arms protectively around herself, she seemed to review the scene from the past. "I grabbed him and held on, tearing his shirt by accident. But he didn't get mad. Instead, he knelt by me and gave me his torn shirt to wear while he was gone. So I wouldn't miss him so much."

As she smoothed the soft white cotton over her legs, she looked like a lonely child. "Usually he was yelling at me for not doing something right, for disappointing him in some way. Giving me his shirt was one of the only tender gestures I remember my dad making. That night I wore his shirt to bed. Then it became a habit. Now men's shirts make me feel safe and warm."

His desire to banish the sad note that had crept into her voice battled with his growing fear that he, too, might disappoint her. "You've got me to keep you warm now."

"Is that a promise or a threat?"

He wasn't ready to make promises. "It's not a threat." Were those tears in her eyes? "Are you okay?"

She sniffed, then blinked "Yep. I'm fine." Suddenly the young girl he'd glimpsed a moment ago was hidden behind an adult facade. "It's just that I never told that to anyone before—and . . ."

"I'm glad you told me."

Even as he said the words, he felt like a jerk. A big jerk. However carefree she pretended to be, she needed someone to depend on. Not someone torn with doubts. The thought of her being with anyone else made a primitive rage surge inside him. But the idea of being tied to his first lover—however wonderful—made him feel trapped, shortchanged. Could it work? Wouldn't he end up feeling cheated? Would he long for the unknown?

Standing on her tiptoes, she kissed him. "I'll see you tomorrow after my class. Just don't write me any more poems, okay?"

Relief washed through him. Maybe he was worrying about things that weren't a problem. The key here was to keep it light. "But I was just getting the hang of it . . ."

"Promise?"

"Spoilsport. Tell you what—I'll drop the poetry writing if you'll go to dinner with me tomorrow."

"It's a deal, Dr. Love."

He grinned wolfishly at her. "Call me when you need another checkup. You seem to be in excellent physical condition, but it never hurts to be sure."

"Yeah, right, Doc." Leaning against the edge of the open door, she regarded him wryly. "You're just a regular good Samaritan, aren't you?"

"I do what I can."

Waving good-bye, he headed for the elevator. He'd had a moment of concern while he had been with Wendy. But she hadn't asked for a decision or a statement of intention, had she? There was no rush.

He began to whistle out loud. When was the last time he'd heard "Whistle While You Work?"

Wendy closed the door behind Jack and leaned against it. A nervous energy coursed through her. Going to the bookcase, she picked up a framed photo of her best friend, Diana, stared at it unseeingly, then put it back down. She took a book off the shelf, opened it at random, but couldn't read. When she looked around the living room, she could only see its faults.

The room was messy, the couch a little lumpy and paint-speckled. The windows that showed a swatch of blue sky needed a cleaning, and the scratched hardwood floor that had initially looked charmingly antique now just seemed battered.

Nothing seemed quite right. She itched to redo it: get a new couch, buy some curtains, refinish the floor. She felt trapped in the apartment she had carefully planned and decorated. Maybe she should just move out. Go to Tahiti or Pago Pago. Flee while she still could.

Stopping herself, she took some deep breaths. It was happening again. This feeling was no stranger—it always came over her when she really started to care for a man. Then she'd freak out and run.

Behind her she heard the door open. Turning, she saw Nathan breeze in.

"Hi, sweets," he said. "What's cooking?"

"Nothing." She plopped down on the couch "Just having a mini nervous breakdown, that's all."

"Tell me everything." He sat next to her, gesturing impatiently for her to remove her feet from the coffee table. "It's Jack, isn't it?"

"You know me too well."

"I thought you two had a great weekend. What happened?"

"I think he's falling in love with me."

He clutched his chest in mock horror. "No! That's terrible! Why, the man is sick!"

"Stop it." She swatted him on the shoulder with one of the couch pillows. "I'm afraid I'm falling in love, too."

"No wonder you're distraught. Reciprocal love. That's enough to make anyone ill."

She shot him a dirty look. "Go ahead, make fun of my insecurities. Laugh at my woes. That's a good friend."

"You're worried it's not going to work out, right?" He knew about her parents' divorce and the pain it had caused her.

"You got it."

"Not every relationship ends in disaster, you know."

"I haven't seen many that don't," she said flatly. Talking about her dad to Jack had reminded her that love too often walked hand in hand with pain and disappointment—and usually walked out.

Tucking a cushion behind his head, Nathan leaned back against the sofa. "Have you told him how you feel?"

"No. He hasn't even said he wants a long-term relationship. It would be a bit hasty, don't you think, to tell him we were destined to crash and burn?"

He chuckled darkly. "Love your imagery, dear. So military."

"This is my life. Can we be serious for a second here?"

"I'm all ears." He didn't look the least bit chastened.

Thinking out loud, she continued, "The whole thing is more

complicated because he was a virgin. The last thing I want to do is let my paranoid thoughts and doubts ruin his first experience."

"Hey, if you can't share with him those revolting parts of yourself that no one else would accept—what's love for anyway?"

"Come on, Nathan." She had to smile even though his words were too close for comfort.

"Okay, okay. It's very noble of you to worry about his first experience, but, honey, don't your feelings count, too?"

"Yes, they do." She patted one of his hands. "I just have this sinking feeling that he's in love with being in love. Not with me."

"Have you asked him if that's what's happening?"

"Of course not. That would be much too simple."

"What was I thinking?" He kept his voice deadpan.

"Besides, what if he said my fears were justified?"

"Gee, I don't know." His voice dripped honey. "Maybe you'd be dealing in reality instead of fantasy."

"That's what I love about you—your bottomless compassion."

A look of exasperation crossed his face. "I don't mean to be harsh, kiddo, but I'm getting lost here. Would you do me a favor and tell me your number one fear?"

Trust Nate to not let her get away with much. That's probably why their friendship had lasted so long. She flashed back to when Jack had asked her about the man's shirt. He'd been attentive, concerned. And she'd trusted him enough to talk about her dad. That had never happened before. "I guess I'm not ready. . . ."

"For what? Happiness?"

"No, to make a commitment."

"Who mentioned commitment?" He snorted. "He's only courting you—with all the finesse of a horny teenager, I might add."

She glanced at the flowers, the crumpled paper with Jack's poems, and the phone he'd called her on several times today. Nathan was right. "Well, then, he's moving too fast."

"You know what? My advice is, enjoy this phase. It passes too quickly. Before you know it, you two will be an old married couple, talking mortgages and nursery school."

A swell of longing moved through her, which she quickly repressed. "Not me. I'm not the kind of woman who gets married."

He rose. *"Chica,* when are you going to overcome this tiresome anxiety about making a commitment and realize there's nothing wrong with you?" When she started to answer, he cut her short. "I don't want to hear any excuses. Accept it: You're lovable. Surely your friends can't all be wrong." With that, he stomped off to the kitchen.

Could it be that simple? Sure, she had friends whom she loved and who she knew loved her. But friends and lovers were not the same thing. She followed him into the kitchen. "I'm sorry. I know I'm waffling, but I'm really confused."

As he rooted through the refrigerator, he said, "The problem is you're kidding yourself."

Uh-oh. He was going to nuke her with one of his annoyingly accurate insights. "About what?"

He turned to stare critically at her, gripping a can of diet, caffeine-free soda in each hand. "In my never-to-be-humble opinion, you're not afraid of a commitment. That was always an easy excuse for running away. But this time it's different. You really like Jack. So much that you're almost tempted to stick it out. *That's* what's scaring you."

"Jeez, you've got to learn to speak your mind, pal."

"Am I right or not?"

Maybe she should listen to her buddy, she thought. He'd been right in the past. "I suppose it's possible."

He leaned against the butcher block, handed her a soda, then popped the top on his own "What exactly happened with your parents' divorce that made you such a chicken poop about falling in love?"

"Good question." She took a sip of the carbonated drink. "I guess it was the way their relationship went from total romance to absolute hatred. They were madly in love . . . at first. They met when my mom was studying ballet. When I was really little, my mom would tell me about the way they met as a bedtime story—her own personal fairy tale."

He interjected with relish, "Starring the honorable Phillip Jorge Valdez?"

"Yep, dear old Dad." She flashed back to being a little girl, cuddling under her blankets, listening to the dreamy voice of her beautiful mother. "Anyway, Mom was dancing a solo part in a show. She saw the heavy doors open in the middle of her dance. From the stage she watched a tall, dark, handsome man slip into a seat in the front row. When she saw the hungry look in his eyes, she almost lost her step. But she would say proudly, 'I kept my cool. Don't give too much away I was taught. I knew my worth.' "

"Love her style," he said. "So Garbo-esque."

"Really, the woman had attitude long before it was popular." With a mix of fondness and exasperation, Wendy recalled her mother's tremendous vanity, which grew stronger as her once perfect life fell apart. "Anyway, to make a long story short, my dad went backstage to meet her. Even though he was fifteen years older—a 'Spanish diplomat in his prime,' as my mom called him— they fell madly in love. When they got engaged, they swore to love each other for the rest of their lives. He gave her a gorgeous engagement ring, telling her not to worry that it was a tight fit. 'It can be adjusted,' he purred. *'Anything* can be adjusted.' "

"Oh, that sounds so dark and threatening!" He smeared peanut butter on a piece of bread, then sliced a banana and arranged it on top. "Does your mom still have the ring?"

She shot him a censuring look. "Are you kidding? She threw it at him when he said he wanted a divorce."

"Bad move. Could have been yours one day."

"Can I finish the story? It turns out he wasn't just talking about the ring being adjusted. Once they got married, he kept trying to make my mom change. Told her she wasn't sophisticated or witty enough. He was very critical of her. And then of me, when I came along. At least once a week I remember sitting hunched over in the dark on the hallway stairs, eavesdropping on their fights. My mom would always burst into tears when he got to the clincher. He'd yell that he never should have married her. That it was the biggest mistake of his life." And in her child's mind, she'd figured she must be a mistake, too. "Then he'd leave, slamming the door behind him."

His green eyes searched hers, then he gave her a quick, hard hug. "Must have been hard for you."

"Yeah. I was nine when they got divorced. It was a relief. I don't ever want to put myself in the middle of that kind of pain."

"You mean you don't want to take a chance on being rejected?"

"I guess that's the bottom line, isn't it?" There it was, the truth she hadn't wanted to see. She bit her lip. Hard. "I just can't forget what my mom always said, 'The hotter the blaze, the more quickly it burns out.' "

He was silent for a moment. "I understand your fears a little better now, hon." Patting her on the shoulder, he added, "But you're not your parents. Take your time. Things might work out with Jack—you don't know yet." He glanced at his watch. "Look, I hate to leave, but I've got an appointment. Do you want me to reschedule it or . . ."

"No, that's okay. I'll be fine. Thanks for listening."

"Anytime, sweets." After grabbing his car keys, he took off.

Alone in her living room, Wendy clutched her arms around herself, savoring the soft feel of the fine man's shirt against her skin. Her muscles ached pleasurably, reminding her of Jack's touch.

The hot fire that burned between them was seductive, enveloping, perhaps even all-consuming. She had survived her family. She didn't know if she wanted to put herself through another trial by fire. Especially when she knew what the ending would be. The chances of love surviving were about as good as a wooden house emerging intact from a raging inferno.

She rose and went to stare out the window that separated her from the teeming world below. Nathan had pegged her accurately. The truth was, she was an emotional coward. Although she would experiment with her furniture, when it came to her heart, she took few chances.

Eleven

The next morning Wendy threw on gray jeans, a billowy white shirt with red collar and cuffs, and a painting smock for her day of teaching. Today she'd have the kids design posters to advertise the services offered by Valencia House. She hoped they'd enjoy the project, plus get the thrill of seeing their artwork put to use. Besides, it would keep her mind off Jack.

Watching the teenagers discover the fun of drawing and painting gave her tremendous satisfaction. She felt, in an odd way, as if she were helping at a group birth—watching fifteen-year-olds struggle to emerge into a world full of new experiences. It gave her a sense of satisfaction she'd never had before.

She checked the clock on the wall. Eight A.M. My God, the sun had barely warmed the pavement and she was already dressed and ready to go to work. This liking-one's-job routine was doing strange things to her life-style. If she wasn't careful, next she'd be jogging with Elsie at the first light of dawn, crying at Hallmark commercials, and drooling over babies in the supermarket.

She had to keep her perspective. This was just a temporary job she happened to like. Not her career. Not her calling. There was no point in getting overly invested in the kids.

Same with Jack. He was a great guy, but she couldn't afford to think of him as a permanent fixture in her life. Jack hadn't said he wanted anything long-term with her. No point in acting the fool.

She'd just slapped some cream cheese on a bagel and filled a cup with coffee when the phone rang.

Nathan's voice came through the receiver, oddly shrill. "Wend, there's been an accident. Someone broadsided my Buick."

An image of a destroyed car and mangled bodies flashed in her mind. "Are you all right?"

"Yeah, yeah."

Relief swept through her. "Thank God."

"I'm just bruised, but Rebecca's hurt."

Wendy vaguely knew Rebecca, another sculptor, who lived in the warehouse next door to theirs. "How bad is she?"

"We don't know yet," he said, sounding dazed. "She's not bleeding, but she can't walk. An ambulance is on the way."

Keep it together, she told herself. He needed her strength right now. "What can I do?"

His voice broke. "Wend, can you come? I think my car's totaled. And I've got to go to the hospital to be with Rebecca."

"Absolutely. Where are you?" She wrote down the address. "I'll be right there."

Checking her watch, she saw that it was eight-fifteen. Depending on how long it took to help Nathan, she might end up missing her class. Wendy dialed the shelter, hoping to reach Mrs. Hughes to let her know about the accident. No answer. She'd have to call later.

Within five minutes she had reached the corner where the accident had occurred and quickly parked her car. Nathan's yellow '56 Buick sat in the middle of the street. Bashed in and listing to one side, it resembled a cartoon car making a hairpin turn. A police car blocked off the street, its flashing lights reflected in the window of a nearby florist shop. A small crowd watched as paramedics lifted Rebecca, strapped to a gurney, into the back of a waiting ambulance. A visibly shaken Nathan stood talking with a balding police officer.

Unbidden, tears filled Wendy's eyes. Life could be so arbitrary, tossing tragedy in the path of an unsuspecting person. It made one feel vulnerable, unprotected.

When she reached Nathan's side, she hugged him. "How did it happen?"

"That lady there ran the red light." He pointed to a young, dark-haired woman who stood in front of a dented van. "I tried to swerve, but there wasn't time. She slammed into the passenger side, so Rebecca got the worst of it. If only—"

"Stop. It wasn't your fault."

His green eyes looked haunted. "But if I hadn't asked her to keep me company while I ran some errands, she'd have been safe at home."

She hated to see her oldest friend racked with guilt over something he couldn't control. She saw that he wanted to make sense of the incident, to find someone—besides mere chance—to blame. What he needed was distraction—and fast.

Taking his arm, she said, "Come on. Let's get your car taken care of, then I'll drive you to the hospital. Rebecca's going to need our help."

At her firm tone, he came out of his self-incriminating haze. "You're right. She's probably in the emergency room, wondering what the hell hit her. Let's go."

Several hours later, Wendy and Nathan returned to their apartment. After settling him in his room with a cup of tea and some magazines, she collapsed back on her bed. She blew her bangs off her damp forehead, then closed her eyes for a moment, savoring the stillness. When her hand lolled over the edge of the bed, Elsie rubbed her wet nose against it and whimpered.

"Oh, Elsie-girl." She patted her dog's graying head. "You need a walk, don't you? But it's going to have to wait till after I catch my breath." Exhaustion swept over her as she reviewed the day's events.

At the hospital, Rebecca and Nathan had been examined and

X-rayed. Rebecca had two broken legs and bruises, but otherwise was okay. Nathan's back was sore, and the doctor had ordered him to stay in bed for a day or two. Wendy had called Rebecca's sister and told her about the accident. Next Wendy called Nathan's insurance company. Then she phoned the shelter, leaving word with one of the teenagers that she wouldn't make her class.

Now she reached out her hand and scratched Elsie's chin. First she had to rest for just a moment, then she'd check in with the shelter. Anyway, her class was long over. Jack would understand. Her eyelids dropped shut.

When she woke with a start, the sky was dark outside her window. Elsie waited patiently at the foot of her bed, a hopeful look on her face. After taking the dog for a quick walk, Wendy hit the play button on her answering machine. While she listened, she picked up the phone to dial Valencia House.

Jack's voice came out of the answering machine. He'd left several messages, his tone changing from one of concern to one of barely repressed irritation. She put down the receiver. His last call had been curt and clipped. "It's five-thirty. Call me."

Grabbing her purse and keys, she headed for Valencia House. It would be better to explain what happened in person. Besides, she ached to feel Jack's arms around her. Her anxieties about whether or not they had a future together could go on hold for the moment. Right now she needed someone *she* could lean on.

Reaching the shelter, she hurried down the empty hall and pushed open the door of his office. From behind his desk, he gave her a cold look, but said nothing. The room and what seemed like a vast emotional distance separated them. Drat. Just when she needed his unconditional acceptance the most, he was sending dagger looks her way.

"Hi." She gave him what she hoped was a charming smile. "I'm sorry about today. . . ."

"Now that I see you're okay," he said, his tone icy, "I have one question. Do you normally cut classes without calling?"

Surprised, she lost her smile. "Didn't you get my message?"

"No."

No wonder he was so steamed. "I'm sorry. I called and left word with one of the teenagers."

"I didn't get any message."

"Let me explain," she began.

"I'm listening." His eyes were flintlike in the twilight.

"There was an accident. A car accident. My roommate and his friend were hurt." She told him what had happened.

"That's too bad." His face didn't soften "Why didn't you call?"

"I *did* call," she insisted, exasperation welling up inside her. Jeez, why was he making her feel as if she'd left her dying mother to go play bingo? "Like I said, once this morning, but no one was in. Then from the hospital. You weren't here, so I left word with one of the kids. Tony, I think."

"You left several kids without a teacher." Rising, he stalked over to the window.

Guilt surged through her. Her students hadn't known she couldn't make class, or why. "Look, I'm sorry."

Turning to face her, he said, "Sorry doesn't change what happened."

She read the disappointment and some other less attractive emotion scrawled across his features. He reminded her of her impossible-to-please father. Didn't Jack ever make mistakes? She'd done the best she could in an emergency. Wasn't she allowed to be human, to be less than perfect?

She asked, "What more was I supposed to do?"

"Insist on talking to Mrs. Hughes or some other *adult*," he snapped. "Or, at the very least, call back to make sure the message got through to me."

"Why? I thought it was taken care of. Besides, as soon as I got home from the hospital, I passed out." She winced at how ditzy that sounded. This was going all wrong. "When I got up I had to take Elsie for a walk because she'd been in the house all day. . . ." Even to herself, she seemed guilty of not taking her responsibilities seriously enough.

"We didn't know you weren't here until Lamar finally told us. We had several teenagers sitting in a classroom for over an hour. Unsupervised. Anything could have happened."

"Come on!" She couldn't believe how unforgiving he was. "It was a car accident! I wasn't out shopping for new clothes. These things happen."

"I'm sorry your friend was hurt, but you have a responsibility to your job." He held himself stiffly, like an avenging god.

How dare he be so righteous? "What would you have me do? Say, 'Oh, sorry, Nate. Let the cops take care of you. I gotta go to work'?"

"Something like that."

What had happened to the warm, tender man she'd spent the weekend with? When he'd told her he had studied to be a priest, she had a hard time imagining it. Now she could easily see him as a guy who liked to set himself above the common person. "You can't be serious."

"Yes, I *am* serious." He strode back to his desk. "You said Nathan wasn't hurt and that you hardly knew the other woman. Couldn't your roommate have taken a taxi home—"

"I can't parcel out my love like that! This was my friend. He needed me. I had to be there."

"Your commitment to your students is more important. Or should be. Missing a class may not seem like much to you, but to them it means you don't care about them."

"But I do care about them. . . ." Couldn't he see how much her students had come to mean to her?

"Then you should have made sure Mrs. Hughes or I knew you wouldn't be here."

Her shoulders slumped as she met the judgment in his stare. Once again she had failed in the eyes of a man who meant a great deal to her. "Okay. I'm sorry I didn't call again. It was really a crazy day, but maybe I could have followed up better." Yeah, in between phoning the insurance agency, chauffeuring Nathan, and comforting Rebecca, maybe she could have conducted a telethon, too. Damn him for making her feel like such a failure. Damn him for making her care.

Tears started, but she blinked them away. Straightening in her chair, she said, "But I won't apologize for helping a friend who needed me."

Jack said nothing for a moment, then let out a deep sigh. His face and voice lost their harshness. "No, you're right. You shouldn't. That's one of the things I like most about you. Your warmth. The way you give of yourself." He came to stand next to her. "Look, I've been unfair. I'm sorry. I've discovered I can be a real jerk sometimes. I'm sorry."

The air between them seemed to quiver. His hand reached out

to take hers. The darkening sky filled the room and made an eerie backdrop for the moment that hovered between them.

She asked, "Why were you so mad at me?"

His hand caressed the skin on her palm. "When you didn't come to class and didn't answer your phone, I got worried. Then angry. I was afraid my first impression of you had been right."

"Your impression that I couldn't make a commitment to the kids," she said dully.

"Right. And if that were true, I'd have to let you go."

Dismay rose inside her like bubbles to the surface of the ocean. Nathan had been right. Things were different this time. Jack had gotten to her on some emotional level—and she'd broken her cardinal rule. She had allowed herself to secretly hope that this relationship could last.

Apparently Jack didn't share that belief. If she messed up in his eyes—which she had to at some point since she was a long way from perfect—then he'd say good-bye. *Hasta la vista.* Take care. And she'd have no one to blame for her pain but herself.

Unaware of her inner turmoil, he pulled her closer. "But I know you take your job seriously. Sometimes I forget that we've got different approaches to life. I overreacted. I'm sorry." He kissed her. "Let's forget it, okay?"

She wanted to respond without reservation to his touch, but a part of her felt wounded.

"Remember, I'm new at this relationship thing." Shrugging, he turned to look out the office window, which showed the encroaching evening fog. "Maybe I'm jealous of your friendship with Nathan."

"Oh, Jack." She smoothed the furrows in his brow, mentally kicking herself for being so self-absorbed. It was easy to forget that this was all uncharted territory for him. "You know Nathan's just a friend. Besides, he doesn't like women. You know . . . that way."

"I figured as much. Maybe I was jealous of how much you care for him."

Did she dare hope?

He ran his hands down her arms and grasped her hands. "I was a jerk. Guess I'm not used to worrying about someone who I've come to l—well, care about."

"Close call." Could he hear her heart pounding? "You almost said that 'L' word."

"Too close for comfort," he said hastily. "I'm not ready for that. Can we put saying it on hold for a while?"

"You bet." She swallowed. Now he seemed to be pulling back, confirming her fears. "If you want, we can wait until we can sing it from the top of Mount Tamalpais." She never went hiking.

"Or holler it down the elevator shaft in the Transamerica Pyramid."

"Or go to Twin Peaks and yell it back and forth."

"We might not hear each other."

"Wasn't that the point?" she asked.

"Maybe." He grinned, unaware that she wasn't joking. "This scares you, too, doesn't it?"

Without waiting for an answer, he wrapped his arms tighter around her. She clung mutely to him, afraid to let him know just how right he was.

Jack watched the smoke curl up from Father Quinn's pipe into the crisp air of early evening. Behind the priest, the sky was a washed-out ammonia blue and the pine trees dipped and bowed in a gentle wind. Jack had told the older man about the car accident and his concerns about Wendy's ability to make a commitment. He hadn't mentioned his own doubts.

"Sometimes," Jack said, "I think I'm worrying about nothing."

Father Quinn's intelligent eyes scanned his face. "Have you considered that your doubts about her might mean something else?"

With a knowledge born of long friendship, Jack waited for the second hit of the one-two punch.

A smile touched Father Quinn's lips. "Wendy is who she is. Her problems—with commitment or anything else—don't really have much to do with you at all." He exhaled slowly. A plume of smoke curled into the air, then disappeared into the encroaching twilight.

"In other words . . ." Jack prompted.

"Perhaps you're seeing a small flaw in her while overlooking a larger problem in yourself."

Jack shifted uncomfortably in his wrought-iron chair. "The old

'And why beholdst thou the mote that is in thy brother's eye, but considerest not the beam that is in thine own eye'?"

"Precisely."

He felt his spirits sink. Father Quinn was no doubt right, but Jack didn't like being in the dark about his own motivations. Still the urge to be right didn't die easily. Jack rationalized out loud. "That sounds good, Father, but if anything, I've been too committed, too responsible all my life. The only thing I couldn't commit to was the . . ."

Light dawned on him, the uncharitable, show-it-all-and-weep sort of light. He looked at Father Quinn, who nodded knowingly.

They spoke at the same time. "The priesthood."

"Right," Father Quinn added softly.

"I see." Jack's mind flew back over the years of pain he'd subjected himself to before he finally admitted that he no longer wanted to become a priest. At the very bottom of his soul, past the reefs of delusion and self-deception, he still felt he'd failed himself and his God. And now he had discovered another dark spot in his psyche. Did he truly love Wendy or was he confusing lust for love? He hated himself for even entertaining the question.

Looking at the diminutive man across from him, Jack shook his head in resignation. "Do we ever really grow up?"

"Truth be told, I doubt it." The priest crossed his pudgy legs at the ankle. "Pass me the sugar cookies, would you?"

Wendy and Nathan spent the following week frantically preparing for their upcoming art show. Whenever Jack called to invite her to dinner or the movies, she told him she was swamped with last-minute work. She felt perfectly justified in saying no. Almost perfectly justified. Rather cowardly. Rotten, in fact.

On Tuesday when she went to teach, he intercepted her in the hallway, his handsome face lighting up. "Hello!" He took her hand. "Where've you been? I've missed you."

"Working." How she longed to surrender to his hungry gaze. But a meltdown always brought radioactive fallout. Especially when she wanted more from him than he seemed ready to give. Better to shut down.

She looked around the hall for someone to distract Jack. No

one. Just when you needed a disturbed adolescent, you couldn't find one. "Look, I've got to get going. I'm meeting Pam before class to help her with her English homework."

"English?"

Good. She'd knocked him off the scent. "Yep. That was my second favorite subject in high school. When she told me she was flunking her lit course, I said I'd help."

"That was nice of you."

No, actually it was selfish. She'd grabbed at the chance to fill her hours so that she didn't have to think about how much she missed Jack's company.

"Gotta run," she said. "See you later."

"I'll call you."

"Great."

Forbidding herself to look back, she walked down the corridor.

Wendy had paint on her nose and epoxy in her hair when her apartment doorbell rang the next evening. Through the peephole she saw Jack. Before opening the door, she checked her reflection in the hand-painted mirror on the wall. She stuck out her tongue. Wendy the scarecrow. Maybe she wouldn't need to make excuses, she'd just frighten him off.

"Hi." She opened the door, but didn't ask him in. "What brings you here?"

Brushing past her, he made himself at home on the couch. This was going to be harder than she'd thought. She followed him.

"Since when do friends, good friends, need a reason to stop by?" he asked.

Why did he have to look so damn sexy when he said that? "It's not that you need a formal invitation, it's just that, um, well . . . you caught me off guard. If I'd known you were coming, I would have cleaned up or something."

"You look fine." He regarded her more carefully. "Sort of."

"I meant," she said with asperity, "that I would've cleaned up the apartment."

"Is this a bad time for company?"

"I always knew you were a smart man."

"Can't you take a break?"

She shook her head. The man was persistent. She had to give him that. Lust could do that to a person.

"I'll come back later."

"Only if you want me to be penniless. Not able to make my rent payment. On the street." She shooed him toward the door. "Or, worse yet, living in your shelter."

"That would be a shame. Of course, then I could offer one-on-one counseling. Late night visits to check on your physical well-being." He raised his eyebrows suggestively. "Daily massages . . ."

"Go on, now." She opened the door and none-too-gently pushed him into the hall. "I really have to get back to work."

"Party pooper." Reaching in through the door, he grabbed her by the wrist. He pulled her against him, then lowered his lips to capture hers.

Surely it couldn't hurt to give in to one kiss. Even a kiss that came on like a polite suitor, then ravished her with the abandonment of a Romeo.

He asked, "Do you know what you're missing?"

"I do." Did he know what it took to ask him to leave?

"I can't change your mind?"

"It's you or my rent payment."

"Go on, make me feel like a heel because I want to be with you."

She couldn't help but smile. "I don't buy you as a martyr."

"I'll work on my delivery. See you later."

" 'Bye."

The door clicked behind him with quiet finality. She'd asked *him* to leave. So why did she feel abandoned?

The more unavailable Wendy made herself, the more romantic he became. First he sent over a set of fine-art brushes she'd once told him she'd kill to have. Then he left sexy messages on her answering machine. When he heard her dog had an outbreak of hot spots, he had a basket of gourmet dog biscuits delivered. She used up a year's supply of thank-you notes trying to keep him satisfied, but at bay.

Next he sent three dozen African lilies and two beautiful men's shirts of the finest cotton. Nathan dragged her into the living room to show her the latest delivery.

He put one hand on a hip. "The boy's technique is getting more sophisticated, I must say."

"Yep, he's a quick study." How long before he graduated to his next relationship?

Her doubts about her relationship with Jack kept mushrooming. Did he love her or the thrill of the chase? What would he do after he caught her, when the relationship fizzled? How long before he decided he was ready for someone new? She had to stop him before she came to care for him too much.

She called him on the phone. "You shouldn't have."

"What—no 'thank you'?"

"Thank you, and you still shouldn't have." It was so easy to fall into light banter with him. So easy to avoid saying what she really felt.

"When am I going to get to see you?"

"I've still got two more tables to paint for the opening tomorrow night."

"Since we live in the same town, this long-distance-relationship routine is for the birds."

"Tweet, tweet."

"Very funny," he said dryly.

"So it was feeble, but I really am swamped." And would be, if she could arrange it, for the next thirty years.

"Then tomorrow after the show, I'm taking you out to a late supper." His voice took on the air of authority he used when he was controlling twenty rowdy teenagers. "Afterwards, we'll go back to my place."

"Yes, sir."

"For a leisurely dessert—al fresco."

"Al's coming, too?"

He paused. "Doesn't 'al fresco' mean in the nude?"

"Hardly." She found herself laughing, some of her tension slipping away. He made her feel so good. Too bad there was no way they'd end up together. "Okay, if I agree to dinner, will you let up on the presents and phone messages?"

"What's the matter, can't take all that attention?"

"I love it, but it's too much. Right now." He didn't need to know that so much attention would always make her feel uneasy.

"Okay. I'll hold off. For now."

"See you at the show tomorrow." That gave her twenty-four hours to plan her good-bye speech.

The phone clicked. Emptiness swept through her.

How would she explain it all to Jack? She could just picture the scene. After the art opening, they'd go to some romantic place for dinner. Taking a sip from her glass of finest Chardonnay, she'd tell him that, yes, she *was* falling in love with him. But since she knew love didn't last—especially for her—she wanted to be the one doing the leaving. After he lobbed a few china plates at her, he'd say that he understood. What a wonderful way to celebrate an art opening! And kill a great thing.

Or she could choose Plan B: move to Borneo, become a chieftain's third wife (not much risk of abandonment there), and send Jack an occasional postcard. Much better.

Friday passed in a blur of last-minute activity. After confirming the caterer's arrival time, Wendy drove to the gallery to drop off the chairs she'd finished the night before. In one corner, Nathan methodically arranged his pieces of sculpture. Wendy conferred with the gallery owner on the best spot for the furniture that Lamar had made. The teenager was going to be thrilled at how great his stuff looked. When everything was set, Wendy returned to her apartment to get ready for the opening.

In her bedroom, she quickly slipped on a flapper-style black dress she'd found a few years before in her aunt's attic. The silly material formed a tight sheath around her torso, showing off her curves. Taking a closer look in the mirror, she wondered if it showed off one too many curves. Might be time to cut back on her health food diet of pizza and doughnuts.

Before an art show, she usually worried about her new furniture designs and the reaction of potential buyers. Tonight all she could think of was Jack. Would she have the courage to do the best thing? And what exactly was that?

She smoothed out the net skirt that began at midthigh and ended just below the knees, donned a pair of slinky black nylons, then stepped into black high heels with rhinestone bows.

There, she looked happy and carefree. No point in signaling her inner turmoil. Her motto: Always dress well when you're about to ruin your life.

Twelve

As soon as Jack entered the old warehouse-cum-art gallery, he saw Wendy. She stood in front of a whitewashed stucco wall, chatting with a man. Her shiny black dress hugged her slim figure and she wore spiky, sexy-looking heels. Lamar and several other teenagers flanked her, like pit bulls guarding their turf. The man leaned in toward her, whispering something in her ear. She laughed and shook her head. Jack could almost feel her dark auburn curls as they brushed the creamy skin of her shoulders.

A rough breath escaped him, causing a pretty black woman to look his way and smile inquiringly. "You okay?"

By conscious effort, he slowed the erratic beating of his heart. "I'm fine, thanks." *Aside from testosterone poisoning and wanting to commit mayhem, I'm doing just great.*

"It's a good show." The woman pointed to the back of the room. "Check out the painted chairs. They'll go fast. Valdez did 'em, and she's hot."

In more ways than you'll ever know. "Thanks for the tip."

Straightening the bow tie on his rented tux, Jack stepped into the milling crowd. From a waiter's silver tray, he snagged a glass of champagne and a puff pastry filled with some sort of melted cheese. Spotting Wendy's roommate, he nodded hello. Nathan sat against the wall beneath some green and yellow blobs splattered on rectangles of poorly stretched canvas.

"Welcome!" Nathan said. "Let me introduce you to Rebecca."

A thin blond woman sitting on a folding chair against the wall tipped her head in greeting. Dark circles rimmed her eyes, and both her legs were in casts. Guilt pricked Jack. The woman from the car accident.

"Rebecca's been telling me how spectacular my work is." Nathan gestured to a sculpture in front of him, then straightened a crease in his wool slacks. "And I've been telling her what an outstanding friend she is."

Jack turned his attention to the mangled piece of iron that squatted uneasily on a block of granite. "It is quite distinct." Distinct from anything he'd ever seen before. Or wanted to see again, for that matter.

"Since I'm feeling magnanimous tonight," Nathan said, "I'll ignore the subtext."

Jack watched the two friends exchange winks. "Thanks."

Rebecca shifted her casts, her grin giving way to a grimace. Jack took another look at Nathan; his skin was ashen, his smile a little forced. The car accident must have been worse than Wendy had let on. Jack had come down awfully hard on her for doing what any good friend would have done. Remembering the scene in his office, he felt terrible. What an arrogant, judgmental ass he could be.

"Excuse me," he said to Nathan and Rebecca. "I'm going to go check out the rest of the show."

"Have fun."

Escaping, he went to stare blindly at a painting. As he sipped his champagne, he pretended to examine the white canvas with several specks of paint hurriedly left in one corner. Why had he blown up at Wendy? Because he'd wanted her love and attention all for himself—even though he harbored doubts about making a long-term commitment to her. Not what you'd call mature.

Across the room, a middle-aged woman with a jutting bosom peered closely at Lamar's chair. "This is really quite nice. How much is it?"

Lamar whispered to Wendy, "What do I do, man?" His voice had a note of terror mixed with elation.

"Excuse us a moment, won't you?" Wendy smiled at the woman. Pulling the teenager close to her, she hissed, "First of all, stop calling me 'man.' "

"Sorry, teach. Jeez, I never thought nobody was gonna buy my stuff." His eyes pleaded with her. "What should I say it costs?"

"Leave it to me." She turned back to the prospective buyer.

"Mr. Washington feels two hundred dollars would be a reasonable price."

Lamar gasped, then covered it with a cough "That's right." Thrusting his hands into his leather bomber jacket, he leaned closer to the woman and raised his eyebrows. "Get it while you can. Price goes up at midnight."

Wendy gently kicked him, then smiled benignly at the older woman. "Did you wish to purchase the chair?"

"Yes, indeed." Without another word, the woman unsnapped her beaded evening bag and extracted a slim leather checkbook and a fountain pen. As she quickly wrote out a check, she gushed, "The chair will go perfectly in my daughter's room. She just adores that—what do you call it?—new wage stuff."

"That's 'new wave,' ma'am." Wendy examined the check, noting that Mrs. Farnsworth's address was on Nob Hill. "We'll have this delivered tomorrow morning, if that's satisfactory."

"Perfect. Thank you so much." She closed her purse with a snap. "You're quite talented, young man."

"Thank you, ma'am"

When the woman walked out of earshot, Lamar let out a yell. "My first sale." He took the check from Wendy and pocketed it. "Two hundred bucks! This is fresh, teach."

"Better than graffiti?" She warmed to the look of absolute glee in his eyes.

"We're talking profit, the almighty dollar." He glanced around the room. "I got to tell somebody."

"How about artistic achievement?"

"What about it?" His caramel-colored eyes found hers.

"Never mind." Turning him toward Pam and Gillian, she gave him a gentle push. "Go share your good news."

" 'Artistic achievement.' Give me a break!" he said over his shoulder. "Don't tell me that selling your stuff don't make you feel good, too."

"You're right." At the very least, these kids would keep her honest. And humble. "It feels great when someone buys your work. Now, go on."

She watched him strut off to tell the others of his success. Even if things were sliding headfirst into the dumpster with Jack, she could feel good that she'd helped her students a little.

Jack watched Lamar walk away, then saw Wendy hurry down the hall and disappear into a back room. He followed her through the open door into the small cubicle. She tucked a business card in her wallet, then stuffed her purse back into a cupboard.

She turned at his greeting. "Hello." Her voice held a note of welcome and some other emotion that he couldn't pinpoint. "Have you been here long?"

"A couple of minutes." He took her into his arms.

Their lips met, her mouth soft and responsive beneath his. He pulled her closer. He probably shouldn't do this, but he couldn't stop. She felt too good. The silky material of her dress slid between his fingers, and her delicate perfume wrapped around him. A discreet cough interrupted them. Annoyed, he looked up to see a smiling woman in the doorway.

"Sorry to butt in," said a small, pudgy redhead, obviously a friend of Wendy's. She held out her arms. "I just had to congratulate you, sweetie."

Jack let go of Wendy.

"Andrea!" Wendy grabbed her friend in a bear hug.

He took a step back. Patience, he told himself.

Wendy turned to him. "I should really get back inside."

"Of course." This was her night to bask in praise. He could wait. He held the door open for her. "Let's go."

"These stupid things don't work." Pam angrily tossed a book of matches on the ground in the alley behind the art gallery. "Let me borrow your lighter."

Lamar handed her an engraved silver box rubbed dull with use.

Flicking it open, she lit her cigarette and inhaled deeply. Then she started swinging her legs, her heavy cowboy boots clanging against the garbage can where she sat. "So I bet you think you're hot stuff now that you sold."

He flicked an ash on the ground. "Girl, you can't sell nothing until you make it first."

Her eyes clouded over with a bottomless rage. "You got a point there, kiddo." She threw her lit cigarette on the asphalt, then jumped down. With her boots, she kicked the butt. "Let's go. We wouldn't want Ms. Valdez to worry about her little teacher's pet, would we?"

Lamar's fists came up, then he shook his head in disgust. "I'm not going to waste my time messing with you. You ain't worth it." Opening the door, he looked over his shoulder. "No wonder you don't have no friends. You're a joke." The door slammed behind him.

She stayed in the alley for a moment, flipping Lamar's lighter over and over in her palm. Then she dropped the silver box into her pocket. "Okay, Lamar, you and your pal are going to pay for this. Nobody treats me like that and gets away with it."

After the show closed, Jack took Wendy to dinner at a small French restaurant on Van Ness Avenue. A classical quartet played in one corner, coaxing every tender nuance from a piece by Mozart. Although nervous, Wendy couldn't help but be charmed. Soft light from sconces flickered across the ornate wallpaper, spilled over the crisp white tablecloths, and highlighted the gleaming silverware. Ivy and red flowers grew in white planter boxes under large windows that overlooked a backyard garden.

Lovely, absolutely lovely, she thought. A romantic place to take someone you cared about. What did he have in mind? Was he going to tell her he loved her? Ask her to "get serious" about him? And what would she do if he did?

As she took a seat, she sighed appreciatively. "How did you ever find this?"

"Stumbled upon it one evening. I loved the food and became friends with the family who owns it." He swung his large form into the booth across from her. "Monsieur and Madame Rathmell still run it, and I have dinner here about once a week."

"With a different woman?" she half joked.

"Hardly. Family style in the front room with the Rathmells."

The waiter brought a bottle of red wine. After Jack approved it, the waiter poured them each a glass. Jack raised his crystal goblet to her in a toast. "Congratulations on your successful art opening."

"Thanks." She clinked her glass with his. "I'm glad you were there."

"Me, too. I've come to like your wild and wacky designs." A lopsided grin on his face, he reached across the table to take her hand. "In fact, I see now that you're a gifted artist."

"Well, thank you." Surprised and flattered, she left her hand in his. "I had the impression that art openings weren't exactly your thing."

"Not my first choice for an evening out," he said. "But I was there because I knew it was important. For *you*."

"You looked as if you were itching to leave."

"I was." He caressed her fingers. "I wanted to be with you. Alone."

Her heart began to pound. Was it possible that he felt as strongly for her as she did for him? That she could finally stop running because she'd found the man she could trust with her heart? "If we keep hanging out together, you'll be going to a lot of art openings."

"I may never love them. That's okay. We can like different things. Makes it more interesting."

A warm glow spread through her.

"Be honest," he continued, "you'd probably yawn your way through the fund-raising dinners I go to for the shelter. Right?"

"Probably."

"Well, I'm not looking for a clone." He cleared his throat and stared down at the table. "Since we're clearing up misunderstandings, there's something I want to tell you."

Seeing how nervous he looked, she felt her heart go out to him. "Yes?" she asked softly.

"When we first got involved, I wanted a long-term relationship." He looked up at her, regret in his eyes. "Turns out I'm not really ready. At least, not yet."

She felt as if she'd been dancing a waltz and suddenly discovered her partner had vanished. Quickly she extricated her hand from his. "Not ready? What do you mean?"

"Don't take this the wrong way. I'm not saying it's over or that I want to leave. . . ."

"Really? What are you saying, then?"

"I need some time. To figure out what I want. We can keep going as we are, as long as you know where I stand."

She searched his eyes, seeing his intelligence, his integrity, his compassion. And his doubts. "This is quite a surprise."

"I know. But I had to tell you the truth. I won't live a lie. I can't. I did that for too long when I was studying to be a priest. It's awkward, but I have to be honest. For you. And with myself."

A part of her appreciated his straightforwardness. A part of her hated him for it. "Thank you for sharing."

"Don't be sarcastic. I'm not telling you this to hurt you."

"It's a little late to worry about that."

"Damn, I'm sorry—"

She cut him off. "Let me see if I understand this. You want to keep seeing each other, both in and out of bed, but with no promises, no plans." Just like other painful relationships she'd been in. "Is that right?"

He fiddled with his linen napkin. "When you put it that way, it sounds terrible."

"I think it is—for me." She knew it was a low blow, but she couldn't stop herself. "Tell me, how does the sexual part jibe with your religion?"

"Don't pull any punches, do you?" His smile faded. "Let's just say I have a lot to sort out."

"And you want me to hang around while you do?"

"Yes, very much."

How could she explain to him—a novice—her conviction that all romantic relationships died a violent death sooner or later? He couldn't know that his words had just confirmed her beliefs. She straightened in her seat. Better a hit-and-run than a slow, lingering death. "I'm sorry, but I can't do that. This is where I call it quits."

"Slow down," he said. "I think you're overreacting. Let's give this a chance."

"After you drop a bomb like that, how do you think this can work?"

"Give it time," he said earnestly. "Give me time."

She looked to the door. Wanted to run as fast and as far as she could. Away from the love she felt. Away from the pain that was washing over her in huge, sickening waves. "Time for what?"

"Time to build what we have. To build something special."

"Right. It's so special, you don't even know if you want it." She couldn't keep the ice out of her voice.

"Cut me some slack, would you? I'm trying not to be a jerk." Wearily he rubbed one hand across his jaw. "Failing, but trying. You're great, Wendy. Everything and more than I ever wanted."

Regret slashed through her. "Then why don't you know if you want me?"

"What can I say? That I met the right woman at the wrong time? That this is still too new? That I don't know the first thing about being in a relationship? That I should have met you a couple of years *after* I lost my virginity?"

Suddenly she understood his real fear—and it got her where she lived. Jack was afraid he'd get stuck with the wrong woman—just like her dad had felt about her mom. "You want more experience, is that it?"

"Yes. Maybe. I don't know. If I never date another woman, will I wonder what I missed? I don't want to make a mistake." Defeated, he dropped his head, running his fingers through his thick, dark hair. "Look, I'm the one with the problem. Not you. I think I love you, but I need to be sure. If I said otherwise, I'd be lying." He held out one hand—palm up—like a peace offering. "Can you understand?"

She tucked her hands into her lap to hide their shaking. How ironic. All her life she'd been afraid of making a commitment—because she hadn't wanted to risk being left. Finally she'd found a man worth overcoming her fears for, and he wasn't ready. Or able. Or willing.

"I do see." She forced herself to speak calmly. "And even though I hate to admit it, I'd probably feel the same way in your position."

"Thank you for that." He let out a deep sigh. "I wasn't looking forward to this conversation—"

"Wait. Please." She steeled herself against the dying hope in his eyes. "I understand, but I don't want a relationship with someone who doesn't know what he wants. It's just asking for pain. I can't do it."

His hands reached across the table to grip the neck of the salt shaker. Better the salt shaker than her, she thought. She shifted uncomfortably on the bench of the restaurant booth.

"I guess I don't have any right to be angry," he said grimly. His dark eyes bored into hers. "Would you rather I'd lied?"

"No. But what did you expect? That I'd say, 'Oh, fine, no problem. I'll hang around until you make up your mind—whenever that is'?"

"I hoped for understanding." He ground the words out. "Patience. Maybe some trust. That you returned my feelings—which I take it you don't."

He'd never know how much she really cared. She'd save that

tiny scrap of pride. Blinking back her tears, she pressed her lips together. "Don't make this so hard. Let's just admit it's doomed. That it can't work. And say good-bye."

"That's it?"

"Yes. That's it." She faked optimism. "You'll find someone else. So will I. It's not the first time and it won't be the last." She didn't know if she wanted to hurt him or not.

"You're going to toss it away?" He drummed his fingers on the table. "Just like that?"

"Yes."

"What was this to you?" The raw note in his voice caused other people in the restaurant to look their way. "A fling, a little game? Take on the virgin?"

"That's not fair." This time she couldn't stop the tears. "It was more to me. Much more." She couldn't tell him she loved him. Not now.

He leaned across the table. "Then why throw it away? Work on it with me. Let it develop."

"So you can really hurt me when you leave?"

"Oh, Wendy, I never said I wanted to leave. Just that I needed time to figure out what I want."

Anger rose inside her. Anger at him for making her hope. Anger at herself for being a fool again. "For such a smart man, you don't get it, do you? Can you say you love me or you want to make a commitment?"

"Like I said, not yet. But—"

She waved her hand dismissively, unable to tolerate any more pain. "Can we go now? Please. I don't feel like eating."

The man she'd grown to love disappeared behind a stranger's mask. He stared hard at her. "Of course, you'll still come to work at the shelter?"

"Yes." Even though she wasn't so sure she was helping tne kids—aside from Lamar—she wouldn't walk out on them, however tempting it seemed right now.

He closed the menu in front of him. Almost instantaneously an attentive waiter appeared at their table.

"May I take your order now, sir?"

Jack gave the barest shake of his head. "We won't be dining after all. The lady's changed her mind."

* * *

Pam bided her time until it felt right. At noon one day when the other kids headed to lunch, Pam walked the other direction down the shelter hallway. Time to act. Reaching Wendy's classroom, she slipped inside. She pushed together several wooden desks, then methodically piled papers on top. As she searched for a can of turpentine, a sound in the hall stopped her. Crouching behind a desk, she tried to slow her quick breathing.

After a moment, the footsteps went away. She pulled Lamar's lighter from her jeans pocket, flicked it on, then touched fire to the four corners of the paper tower she'd built. As the orange tongues of flame began to curl the edges of the paper, she kneeled to watch. For the first time that day, she smiled.

The flames licked higher. She stretched her hands out to the warmth, then rose slowly. After dropping the lighter to the floor, she savagely kicked it into the corner. A turn of the knob and she was back out in the empty hall. No smoke followed her. Piece of cake. Whistling under her breath, she headed to the dining room for a burger and an alibi.

Jack threw a clean towel over his shoulder, then grabbed the basketball. The night before he hadn't slept well, and now he didn't feel like eating lunch. Maybe shooting a couple hundred baskets would let him forget the dull throb that came with every thought of Wendy. Her tanned, smiling face flashed in his mind. Shooting baskets probably wouldn't do it; she wasn't easy to forget. But he didn't have any other brilliant ideas.

As he turned a corner, his eyes began to water. What was that smell? Scanning the hall, he saw a white plume of smoke escaping from under the door to Wendy's classroom. Smoke. Fear gripped him. Her room was on fire.

He yanked the fire extinguisher off the wall, then gingerly laid his fingers against the door. The scratched wood was cool; the fire must be young—maybe he could still put it out. He stepped inside. A tower of flames burned in the center of the room, consuming the last remnants of the old desks. Thick smoke billowed toward the open door. Pointing the fire extinguisher, he sprayed the desks and papers. As soon as he put the fire out in one spot, flames sprang up someplace else. Smoke stung his eyes, making him cough. He resisted the desire to run to find more help. He had to stop the fire now, or it would move on to the rest of the shelter.

Finally, after several minutes, he put out the last flame. Smoke mushroomed into the air. Wiping the sweat from his eyes, he retreated to the clean air of the hallway. He leaned against the wall and tried to catch his breath. Jeez, that had been close. The shelter—and with it his dreams for the kids—could have been destroyed. Thank God he'd gotten there in time. He couldn't have taken another loss. Wendy saying good-bye had been plenty.

A hand on his shoulder made him jerk up his head. Wendy stood in front of him. Concern etched itself across her delicate features. Without thinking, he reached out to pull her against him, to feel the sweet comfort of her body. Then he stopped. He'd blown it—thrown away that right. His arms dropped to his sides. The dull pain—his new companion—returned.

"Are you all right?" she asked, her normally melodious voice edged with fear.

"Yeah, I'm fine." Just fine.

"What happened?"

"Someone tried to torch your classroom." The smoke and dust eating at his throat made him cough again.

"Arson?"

"I'm afraid so."

"This really disturbs me," she said, shuddering.

He couldn't kiss away her fears. Not anymore. "Try not to worry. I'll take care of it." He patted her on the shoulder, telling himself that she needed the human touch. "Class'll be canceled until we clear this up. I'll call you if I find out anything."

When he walked back in the room, he wasn't surprised that she followed. Wendy didn't give up easily—until she felt like it. Then she bolted.

She gasped as she looked around the room. "Who would do this? And why?" She pulled her jacket tightly closed as if to protect herself from the knowledge that this fire was no accident. "Maybe I don't belong here. Maybe teaching is a mistake."

"No, you're a good teacher," he said. "But there's nothing you can do here. Go home, Wendy."

"I can't go. Someone set this fire in *my* room. It's a message to me."

He didn't disagree, but he'd do almost anything to save her from the dread and outrage he heard in her voice. "Don't forget, we're only speculating it's arson."

She didn't buy it. "What else could it be? First someone trashes my classroom, then Lamar writes graffiti all over my kitchen. Now this. What if it was . . ."

They both spoke at once. "Lamar."

"It doesn't make sense," she said. "He's been doing great. Why would he be angry at me?"

"I don't know." He had to distract her—get her mind off her fear. "I'm going to clean up the paper and sweep a little. If you want to stay, I could use your help."

"Thanks. I'd feel better if I did something."

In silence they cleaned up the room. She crouched and started to pick up the burnt paper, tossing it in the garbage can. As Jack knelt to help her, he tried not to think about brushing the smudge of soot from her temple or kissing away the lost expression on her face.

Before he had touched her for the first time, he'd had no idea what he was missing. Now he knew. Too well. Being with her had been so much better than any dream, any naive fantasy. And he'd thrown it all away—for what? So he could be free? Free to look at other women and realize they didn't appeal to him because they weren't Wendy? Free to realize what a selfish, immature jerk he'd become?

"Oh no!" she said, interrupting his thoughts. "Look."

He stared at the cigarette lighter in her hand. "Guess it *was* arson."

"Worse than that." She turned the dull silver box over in her hand, tracing the engraved art deco design. "This is Lamar's."

His heart sank. Anybody but Lamar. Since Wendy had been working with the teenager, the boy had changed, opened up, found something he was good at. If he'd torched Wendy's room, it would be a terrible blow. To everybody. "We've got to talk to him."

"I can't believe he could do this," she said, her voice breaking.

"We don't know that he did yet." A sickening throb started in his gut. Despite all he'd seen, he still lost a part of himself when one of his kids stepped over a line. "I'll find him. Meet me in the conference room in twenty minutes."

Lamar sprawled back in the stiff wooden chair, glaring at Jack and Wendy. "I didn't do it."

"We're not saying you did," Wendy said. "We just need to ask a couple of questions." She watched him closely. Gone was the talkative, confident teenager. In his place was a sullen, resentful boy whose sneer hid his pain. "Do you know how your lighter ended up in my classroom?"

He clamped his lips together in anger. "How the hell do I know?"

"Come on, Lamar," Jack said. "There was a fire, we found your lighter. You wrote graffiti in Ms. Valdez' apartment. It's logical that we ask you some questions."

A rustle at the open door of the conference room caught Wendy's attention. Turning, she glimpsed frizzy blond hair and a pale face, then the eavesdropper was gone. Had it been Pam? Wendy looked back just in time to see Lamar lunge out of his chair, knocking it to the floor.

"I don't have to answer your stupid questions!" he yelled. "I didn't set no fire."

Hope surfaced in her heart. Maybe they'd been wrong after all. "Lamar, wait a second—"

"You wait, *teach*." He ground out his words, his face a mask of anger and hurt. "All that phony stuff about 'Oh, you're such a good kid, Lamar. You're really talented. Keep trying.' It was just lies, all of it, lies."

"That's not true. I meant every word." She tried to put her arm around him, but he jerked away.

"Sure. That's why you think I set your room on fire. You're just like everybody else. Treating me like I'm nothing. Well, nothing from nothing leaves—"

"Hold it right there, son." Jack rose. "Before you say something you regret."

"Yes, sir, *Mister* O'Connor." Lamar spat out the words. Then, taking his hair pick from his pocket, he deliberately took his time in combing his hair. "Time for me to hit the streets. This place ain't no shelter. It's just another cage." He headed for the door.

What had she done? Doubt assailed her. With each week, it became clearer that she wasn't good at this teaching stuff. Now her blundering had really hurt one of her best students.

"Lamar, please, wait!" She started after him.

Jack caught her and held her back. "Let him go."

"I can't." She struggled to get free of his arms, but he wouldn't release her. Her heart was breaking again. This was all her fault. She couldn't do anything right. "Let me go! I've got to talk to him."

"It won't do any good. He can't hear you now. I'll talk to him later."

"What if he does something stupid because he's so angry and hurt? He's just a kid. . . ."

"A savvy kid. He'll be okay till I talk to him."

Jack pulled her against his body in a warm hug, but his strength couldn't comfort her. It only reminded her of what she couldn't have. And now Lamar was gone, too. Why had she thought confronting the teenager would work? Once again she'd discovered how lousy she was at emotional relationships.

Tears welling up in her eyes, she stepped out of Jack's arms. She was a danger to the very kids she was here to help. She didn't know enough about how to handle them. She thought of the burned remains of the students' cheerful, exuberant paintings. It had been a novel experiment, but she'd failed.

"I think," she said, "it's time for me to leave."

The smile he gave her was warm, understanding. "Okay, I'll call you when the room's fixed up again."

He didn't get it.

"No," she said. "I mean I can't teach here anymore."

Thirteen

"What?" Jack heard anger jump-start in his voice. "You can't quit. Think of how your kids will feel if you just take off."

"Believe me, I *have* thought about it." She moved her shoulders as if she were shifting a weight she'd been carrying for a long time.

"Trust me, my leaving will be best for everyone. When I first came here, I thought I could help a few kids. But now I see that I'm only making things worse."

Oh, now he understood. The vandalism, the graffiti, and then the fire in her room had gotten to her. Poor kid. Working with volatile teenagers was exhausting, particularly for someone without experience. As he looked at her tightly held figure, his anger left him. She needed reassurance—not to mention a good back massage. Hold it, pal. You blew your chances in that department. "Look, if it's the fire, we'll get it all straightened out—"

"It's more than that. It's what happened with Lamar. I've thought a lot about it, and I don't believe he set the fire. But it's too late. I've already accused him." She held up her hands in a gesture of defeat. "I can't do this job. Let me go before something more important than a room gets ruined."

"I didn't know you felt that way."

"Well, now you know."

Weariness hit him, threatening to knock down the walls he'd built to separate himself from the pain of her good-bye. Here was a new wrinkle in his angst. If he was honest, he'd admit he'd cut his sense of loss with the knowledge that he'd see her at the shelter. But if she quit teaching, what would he have left? The freedom he'd thought was so crucial?

Looking up at the ceiling, he clenched his fists, dimly noting the bite of his fingernails into the skin of his palms. Every cell told him to fight. To hang on to Wendy with all his strength. But he couldn't make her stay if she wanted to go.

His eyes were drawn back to the compelling planes of her face. Longing slammed into him again. Until he had to look away. "It's your decision," he said finally.

"I'm sorry."

Not as sorry as I am.

"This job isn't for everyone. You have to want to be here." They were the right words, but his heart wasn't in them. "I wish you the best."

"Thank you. For you, too. Good-bye." She picked up her purse. Her heels tapped on the floor as she headed out of the conference room.

At the door, she stopped to look at him. A tentative smile on her lips, she seemed about to say something. A curt wave was the best he could do. Her smile faded, and she left.

Numbness gripped Wendy as she hurried, head down, toward the front door of the shelter. If she could get outside without falling apart, she'd at least save the rest of her tattered pride. She didn't see Lamar until she almost slammed into him. He was still here! Thank God.

"Lamar, I'm sorry about what happened—"

"Never mind that, teach," he said. "Pam ran away."

"What? Why?"

"She didn't say—just told me she was splitting. If we take off now, we might still catch her."

"My van's out front," she told Lamar. "Let's go."

After several hours of searching the back alleys south of Market, Wendy stopped for dinner at the drive-up window of a fast-food restaurant.

"Two chicken sandwiches," she told the big plastic head, "a cola, and a coffee, please."

After paying for the food, she passed some to Lamar. He wolfed down his share in record time while she kept driving, nursing her weak coffee. She hadn't said anything about the fire in her room, but somehow as the search wore on, the rope of trust was reweaving itself between them.

Stopping at a red light, she turned to ask, "Where to next?"

"Broadway." The teenager referred to a seedy patch of strip joints in North Beach, bordered by the Italian district on one side and Chinatown on the other. "Let's check the clubs."

"But Pam's underage." Shifting into first gear, she slowed down to bump across a cable car track. "She can't get into a club, can she?"

He stared out the dusty window at the purple bruise of twilight. A red streetlight cut through the incoming fog, casting an unreal glow on his face. "Get real. It's easy for a teenage girl to get into a club—even a homely chick like her." His teeth flashed in a sharklike grin.

"You've had to grow up awfully fast, haven't you?"

"Yeah," he said, his cocky attitude slipping for a moment. "But it's cool. When I sell my line of furniture, I'll be driving some hard bargains."

"*Line* of furniture now? Getting big ideas, aren't we?"

"Didn't you tell me to believe in myself?"

Barreling out of the tunnel, she left an echo of horns behind her. "You're right. Your own line of furniture is a great idea. After we find Pam, I'll help, if you'd like."

"Great!" he said. "Maybe after class."

Here was the moment she'd dreaded. "You know, I won't be teaching at the shelter anymore."

There was silence for a moment. "You're leaving?" He stared straight ahead, not making eye contact. "Well, didn't take you long to get tired of us."

"I'm leaving for personal reasons. Not because I'm tired of anybody." He still wouldn't look at her. "If you want my help, you can work at my studio after school." She was surprised at how quickly the offer came to her lips. Her relationship with her students made her feel needed, connected . . . valuable.

"You're on." For the first time that night, the teenager's smile was genuine.

Up ahead, the lights of Broadway glittered in the fresh evening air. After finding a parking space, Wendy and Lamar headed for the clubs. Crowds of people strolled along the sidewalk.

From the dirty stoops of strip clubs, barkers yelled out descriptions of the women inside. Every once in a while a barker flicked open a tattered velvet curtain to reveal a smoky interior. No sign of Pam in any of the clubs.

Lamar turned down a dark street. "Come on."

"Where are we going now?" she asked, not thrilled at the thought of leaving the main drag.

"To Washington Square. Sometimes kids crash there."

Lamar strode ahead of her, his shoes echoing on the poorly lit, empty sidewalk. She wished she'd parked the van closer so they'd have a means of escape if they needed one.

As they passed a street that dead-ended at the square, an old Chevy screeched to a halt next to them. Several young men in baseball caps turned backwards, high-top tennies, and black clothes hopped out. They whistled. It took her a moment to realize they were whistling at her. Oh, great, just what she needed, a band of sex-starved hoodlums.

When she looked around for Lamar, he'd disappeared.

Walking faster, she ignored the men. Pretending to see someone she knew across the park, she waved her hand. It was hokey, but worth a shot. The footsteps sounded closer behind her. She turned quickly in to the park, her shoes sinking in the damp grass. A group of kids in front of her parted, wary looks on their faces as they stared over her shoulder. Suddenly, from behind, someone grabbed her arm and spun her around.

Terror washed over her, followed by the ice-cold knowledge that this could get ugly real fast. She glanced at the kids on sleeping bags near her. They watched eagerly, as if this were a particularly exciting TV show. No help there. Lamar was still nowhere in sight. Not that it mattered—she couldn't let him go up against five guys. She'd have to take care of herself.

Smiling sweetly, she began to back up. "Another time, guys."

"Not a chance. Tonight's the night."

She kept walking backwards towards Columbus Avenue, where there were lights and people. Maybe a passing cop would see her. If not, she could run into traffic. A close encounter with a car would be better than a head-on with the guys facing her. Taking their time, the punks came after her. Suddenly her back slammed into a solid wall of muscle.

"Oomph!" she said.

"That's enough, boys." A wonderfully familiar voice rang in her ears. "The lady's with me." Jack's hand firmly gripped her arm.

She looked up, her eyes drinking in the strong lines of his face. "Oh, thank God!"

When he glanced down, his dark blue eyes softened momentarily. Then he turned back to the young men, his face a cold mask.

"You willing to fight for your 'lady'?" The leader took a step forward. He fished in his pocket for something. A knife?

Jack didn't flinch. "I won't have to, because you're leaving."

"And soon, joker," someone said.

"You tell him, Mr. O'Connor."

"Back off, fools, while you got the chance."

What was that? Wendy turned to find the source of the chorus.

Almost the entire parkful of teenagers—including Lamar—stood behind Jack, cheering him on. Some had knives, others broken bottles. She only had a moment to wonder where Lamar had been before her attention was drawn back to the confrontation in front of her.

The five young men began doing a backward shuffle. "Sorry, man."

"Our mistake."

"Who *is* that dude, anyway?"

Pivoting, they took off running across the wet grass and out of the park.

Jack turned and smiled at the crowd of teenagers. "Thanks, guys."

"Payback time, Mr. O'Connor." One of the young women gave him the high-five sign. "You look out for us, we look out for you."

While Wendy had known that the kids at the shelter looked up to Jack, this moment made it clear that his influence reached far beyond Valencia House. To the street kids he was a well-known defender of their rights. And they were ready to back up their feelings with actions.

Now that the danger had passed, she felt her adrenaline level crash. A deep shudder ran through her body. How close she'd come to disaster! If Jack hadn't shown up, what would have happened? She didn't want to think about it. What she wanted to do was thank him, but without fifty kids as an audience. She waited as the teenagers slowly wandered off until only Lamar loitered behind.

"Way to go, Ms. Valdez!" Lamar said, shaking his fist in the air. "Don't let nobody mess with you."

"Thanks, Lamar. Where did you take off to anyway?"

He looked chagrined. "Sorry about that. I thought I saw Pam run behind the church. I was trying to catch her."

"It's okay." She turned to thank Jack.

Jack cupped her chin, his eyes scanning her face. "Are you okay? Did those creeps touch you?"

"No, but I think you just saved my life."

"I'm glad I got here when I did."

"Me, too. Although 'glad' has got to be the major understatement of the year."

He laughed softly, then asked, "What were you doing here anyway?"

As she told him, the fear overtook her again. All she wanted was to collapse against the firm length of his torso. Her body swayed toward him.

"Oh, baby." Jack caught her and drew her against him, holding her fiercely.

The terrible fear began to ebb out of her. "I was afraid. So afraid."

"Hush." He smoothed a hand gently down her hair. "You're safe now. I won't let anybody hurt you."

Reluctantly she stepped back. "How'd you find us? Your timing was perfect."

"A lucky fluke. When I heard Pam and Lamar had run away, I came here first."

"Wait a sec!" Lamar said indignantly. "Did you say run away? I wasn't running, I was *helping* look for that bimbette."

"I know that—now." Jack smiled down at the lanky teenager. "But you forgot something. Something important. We're a team at the shelter. Next time let me know first, okay?"

"Okay, Mr. O'Connor, but time was of the essence, you know?"

"Doesn't matter. We're in this together."

We're in this together. Jack's words echoed in her mind. He really meant them—and she could see he'd broken through another one of Lamar's defenses. What would it be like if she and Jack were a team? Longing washed over her. She'd never get the opportunity to find out.

Up until now she'd seen commitment to another person as dangerous, destined to end in pain, like her parents' marriage. For the first time she saw intimacy with another face, the face of mutual love and trust: passionate but tender, willing to give as well as take. How sad to finally see what could be—and to know she couldn't have it with Jack. That he didn't want that commitment from her.

"Hey, Mr. O'Connor," Lamar said. "We'd better hustle if we're going to find Pam—"

"Hold it. It's time for you to go back to the shelter."

"No way! I wanna help."

"You have. But think about it. If one of Pam's peers is there, she might not back down."

"Oh." The teenager paused. "I see what you mean. Okay, take me back."

Watching the exchange, Wendy marveled again at Jack's deft touch. While firm, he showed the kids love and respect—and they opened up like sea anemones when the predators had left. The more she knew about him, the more she loved him. And the more bitter her loss felt.

Together she and Lamar drove back to the shelter while Jack followed in his pickup truck. After turning the teenager over to the housemother, Jack and Wendy took off again in search of Pam.

Wrapping her purple wool sweater around her, Wendy snuggled up in the cab of his pickup. The front seat was a cozy island in the dark, foggy night. How she wished they were together for some other reason besides going on a rescue mission.

Deal with reality, not fantasy, she told herself. Jack was not hers and never would be. The only solace was recognizing that she'd grown up a little. Because of their relationship, she had discovered she was willing to love and to risk the pain that came with opening her heart. Letting Jack go was like cutting off a part of herself. Yet she knew she deserved more than he could offer her right now.

Pride rose inside her. It was time to get on with her life. Time to let the healing start. But first she had some apologizing to do.

She reviewed their last argument, feeling the hot flush of embarrassment move up her face. When he'd told her his honest fears, she'd freaked out. She'd been rude, immature, and defensive. Pushed him away. She'd behaved terribly.

Just exactly how did one eat crow, anyway?

He turned down Powell Street and headed for Fisherman's Wharf.

"I was so glad when you showed up at the park tonight," she said.

"Me, too." Briefly he turned to her, his eyes teal pools in the half-light.

She had to do what was right—however uncomfortable it made her feel. "I've been thinking," she said, "and, well, I have to apologize for being an emotional coward."

"Are you talking about what happened with Lamar?" The car bumped over the pitted asphalt of another empty alley. "Or with us?"

That's it, go for the jugular. "I'm talking about our conversation at the restaurant. You were honest about your doubts, and I freaked out. I'm sorry."

He looked both ways before crossing an intersection where drunken patrons streamed out of a noisy pub. "Don't apologize. It was awkward all around."

"I know, but I overreacted. And I figured out why."

"Oh?" His tone said he was politely interested, nothing more.

"I've always been afraid of getting emotionally close to a man and letting him get close to me."

"Why were you afraid?" The streetlights flickered across the strong lines of his face, giving no clear clue to his feelings.

"Remember I told you that when I was a teenager I didn't fit in, I felt as if nobody liked me, and that I didn't get along with my dad—all that stuff?"

He nodded.

"I know it sounds melodramatic," she said, "but I thought there was something terribly wrong with me. I didn't want anybody to get too close—because I was sure he wouldn't like the real me." She stared blindly out the window. "The me I usually keep hidden."

"Sounds painful."

"It was. So I always kept men at a distance, never got very involved."

"Then I come along, we get involved, and I tell you I don't want a long-term relationship," he said. "That must have hurt. I'm sorry."

"I don't want your pity, Jack. I want to thank you."

"Thank me?" He waited at a stop sign while a bent-over woman carefully negotiated the crosswalk.

"Sure, you did me a favor. Inadvertently, but a favor."

He quirked an eyebrow. "How?"

"Well, I had to look at myself honestly. And I didn't like what I saw. I saw that I was so afraid of being rejected, I always ran. When you told me your doubts, I flipped. And did what was comfortable—run. When my classroom at the shelter was torched, I did the same cowardly thing." She tried to slow down, but the words kept tumbling out. "When Lamar asked me to help look for Pam, I felt he'd given me a chance to redeem myself. Do you know what he plans to do?"

"No, what?"

She tucked her boots under her on the front seat. "Start a line of his own furniture. I was so impressed with him when he said that. That's when it hit me. Here's this kid who's had a terrible life and he's got the courage to hope. To trust in himself—whatever the future brings. Can you believe it?"

"The kids are amazing, aren't they?"

"Absolutely." She looked at his face, hoping he understood. "Then I saw how I'd let my fears stop me. And I decided to kick them out. So you see, I really owe you one—for helping me change for the better."

He pulled the car over to the curb and turned to face her. Behind her, an orange neon sign on a twenty-four-hour check-cashing store flashed on and off. "Do you know that you're delightful? The real you."

"You think so?"

"I know so. You're wonderful."

"Hold on, let's not slip into hyperbole," she said. "Blanket positive statements like that make me feel I have to give you a road map to all my faults."

"You're too hard on yourself."

"No, I'm *not* wonderful," she insisted. "No one can live up to that. I'm okay. I mean, sometimes I'm better than just okay, but I'm not, you know, I wouldn't say I was wonderful." Argh! Why did she have to sound like a Valley girl when she was nervous?

He turned off the ignition. "Listen. I said you were wonderful. Not perfect. There's a difference."

"Are you saying I'm not perfect?" This felt romantic to her. Did he have a change of heart?

"Okay, okay, you're perfect. To me." He shifted his body so he could lean back against the driver's door.

A warm glow spread through her. "My God," she said, her voice breaking. "I just reveal the part of me that embarrasses me the most, the part that's cowardly, self-pitying, and needy. And you tell me I'm perfect?" Wiping away her tears, she laughed. "That qualifies you for sainthood in my book."

"No, anything but that."

"Why?" She looked up at his cynical tone, wondering what his shuttered look hid. "Don't you want to be deified?"

"Not anymore. That's been *my* Achilles' heel. Accepting my

limitations, settling for being just a man with failings like everybody else."

She had a sudden glimpse into the room where his personal
anguish was caged. "Are you still upset with yourself for not becoming a priest?"

"Sure." He turned to stare through the front windshield at the
inky night studded with skyscrapers. "When I quit seminary
school, it made me question whether I could keep my commit-
ments. Made me wonder if I knew myself at all."

"You just changed your mind about what you wanted to do," she
said gently. "That's allowed. Let yourself off the hook, would you?"

"I could say the same thing to you." Jack's eyes scanned her
face. She was so close, he could reach out and pull her against
him. If he knew that she wanted that as much as he did. "Isn't that
funny? We've both been wrestling with parts of the same question.
Probably why we're drawn to each other."

"We are drawn to each other, aren't we?"

"You bet." He heard the hopeful note in her voice. Was there a
chance for them after all? "When I had doubts about my readiness
to commit to you, I couldn't handle them. I wanted to keep all my
options open." He looked at her, embarrassed to admit his frailty,
his need. "But I've been alone for a little while now. Being without
you feels miserable, not like freedom. I don't like it."

"Are you sure? I mean, I can understand why you'd want more
experience. That's only normal."

"After you said good-bye, I thought about it a lot." He resisted
the urge to clench his fists. "I realized that you fall in love with a
person. An individual. Not a body. Not a face, or a hairstyle. Not
even sex—although it's great. And when the right person comes
along, you say, 'Thank you.' You don't say, 'Come back later. This
isn't the perfect time.' " He kept his eyes straight ahead. Here was
the place where she could say good-bye again—if she wanted to.

"How did you get so smart so quickly?"

"I had a good teacher," he said. Turning, he watched as her
sweet face broke into a grin.

"We both learned something."

"What if those creeps had hurt you tonight? What would I have
done?" He couldn't stop himself. He had to touch her. With his

index finger, he traced the shape of her lips. "I want you. Not anybody else. Only you."

Tears showed in her eyes. His heart opened.

"You can't know what those words do to me," she said. "I thought I was going to apologize for my tacky behavior, then never see you again. Instead, you tell me all these wonderful things. Things I thought no one would ever tell me."

So this was intimacy, he thought, feeling a hard joy in his chest. Trusting the other person enough to be yourself. And getting the same freedom back. Heady stuff. He was silent for a moment. Then, linking his fingers with hers, he said, "For the first time, I know unequivocally that I made the right decision about leaving the seminary. This is what I wanted."

"I didn't know what to do without you," she said, her voice breaking.

Tenderness rushed through him as he looked at her tear-streaked face. "After you ended it, I felt lost. Not free, not relieved. Cut adrift."

"Really? You're so strong, sometimes it's hard to believe you need anybody. Least of all me."

"I do. Believe me." He watched her expression soften and knew he'd come home. "Someone who loves me. Someone who won't push me away when she sees my demons."

"I'm honored that you trust me—"

Before she could finish, a rapping at the window interrupted them. Out of the gloom emerged the weathered face of a street person. "Hey, buddy," the man rasped, "can you spare five bucks?"

"*Five* bucks?!" Jack exclaimed. "What for?"

The man grinned, revealing yellowed teeth. "I gotta send a fax to Mom."

"Prices have gone up," Wendy muttered.

"Sorry, pal." Jack shook his head. "Can't help you."

"I'm shocked." She watched the man stumble away. "I thought for sure you'd give him some money."

"Lesson six in urban living. Never open your window to a stranger at two in the morning. It's hard to help anyone when you're dead."

He switched on the ignition and turned to Wendy. "Look, we're going to have to handle this later. We'd better get going again if we want to find Pam."

"Sure. We can finish talking later." Her questions weren't going anywhere. They'd be there in the morning.

Several more hours passed with no luck. They scoured the wharf, the business district, and the South of Market area. Finally dawn edged itself next to the sleeping city. Checking her watch, she saw that it was six-thirty. "Can we stop for coffee? I'm fading fast."

"Sounds good." Spotting a doughnut shop, he pulled into the parking lot. "I'll be right back."

Inside, he ordered and slid two dollars across the cheap plastic counter. A young man in a battered white cap poured steaming java into two Styrofoam cups.

Suddenly Wendy dashed in through the open door. "Jack, hurry! I just saw Pam go in the alley."

Together they ran behind the shop. Unaware of them, the teenager busily rummaged through a Dumpster. Relief swept through Jack. Although a little dirty, she didn't look bad for having spent a night on the streets.

"Hi, Pam." Carefully he approached her. "We've been looking for you."

The girl swung her head around. "Pat yourself on back, Sherlock." She stepped away from the metal container and began backing down the alley. "Now, get lost!"

He stopped. Pam had always been difficult to handle, pushing away anyone who might give her the love she needed. "Come back with us. We can talk after you've gotten some rest."

"No way. I'm not going back. And nobody can make me."

"No one's going to force you to do anything. We're worried about you. Lamar told us you took off—"

"That narc!" Clenching her fists at her sides, she whirled toward Wendy. "Let me guess. He told *you,* right? Teacher's pet goes right to his little protector." Turning, she stomped off down the alleyway.

Wendy followed. "Wait. Lamar's not my pet."

"Yeah, right. And Madonna sings opera."

Wendy reached the teenager's side. "Is that what's bothering you? You think I like him more than you?"

"I don't need a neon sign to tell me I'm not wanted."

"Oh, honey," Wendy said, pulling Pam's stiff body into a hug, "of course you're wanted. I care about you. Would I have looked all night for you if I didn't?"

On the sidelines, Jack held his breath. This was the crucial moment. It could go either way. With all his heart he hoped Pam wouldn't push Wendy away. They both needed this reunion.

Wendy's voice radiated calm conviction. "I'm not going to let you go until you agree to come back. Until you see that I care about you."

"Let me go," Pam said, struggling.

"I'm not going to let you go. I care about you too much."

Finally the girl's body slumped. Tears began to spill down her face. Watching, Jack let himself breathe normally again.

"You won't want me back when you know what I did," the girl sobbed.

"Yes, I will."

Pressing her lips together tightly, the teenager shook her head. "No, you won't. I'm the one who tore up your room the first time. Then yesterday morning, I set the fire and left Lamar's lighter. I wanted to get him into trouble 'cause you liked him better. And I wanted you to like me. See, I'm bad. I'm not a sweet little kid. I'm no damn good. Just like my mom always said."

A loving look in her eyes, Wendy wiped the tears off the girl's grimy face. "Honey, you're not bad. You've done some things that aren't good, and that has to stop. Come back to the shelter. So we can work it out."

"I can't believe you don't hate me."

"Believe it." Draping an arm over the girl's slumped shoulders, Wendy turned toward the car. "Now let's go. We can talk later. After we get some rest."

Behind him, Jack watched Pam meekly climb into the backseat. Wendy had just pulled off a miracle.

After getting Pam safely settled in at the shelter, Jack drove Wendy home. He stopped the truck in front of her apartment building. He turned to her, hating the thought of leaving, but not wanting to assume too much. Although she'd stopped pushing him away, did that mean she wanted him back in her life? In her bed? She hadn't said so.

"Come upstairs," she said softly.

His heart lurched. In expectant silence, they took the elevator up to her apartment. The Doberman greeted them at the door, pressing her wet nose into his hand. Then, happy to have her people home, the big dog curled up at the foot of the sofa and went to sleep. Nathan's door was open and his room empty. A few slivers of sunlight pierced the closed miniblinds, hitting the hardwood floor of the nearly dark apartment.

She turned to him. "Would you hold me?"

"Mmmm." The deep sound escaped from him as he folded her soft, curved body against him. She felt so right. "You did great tonight, my love."

She rubbed her cheek against his jacket. "What a night! I'm exhausted."

He didn't want to ask, but he made himself. "Should I go?"

"No, please. I want you to stay. I need you."

Tilting her head back, he covered her face with kisses. Touch sparked touch until a fire raged between them. Laughing as they struggled with buttons and straps, they tore off each other's clothes. In the chilly air of morning, they stood naked—happy as two children doing something deliciously forbidden.

"Let's go in my bedroom," she said.

Lifting her in his arms, he carried her into her room.

First with his eyes, then with his lips, he blessed every tender inch of her. "You feel so silky, so good. I missed you."

"Me, too," she said.

Wendy felt his caresses connect with her on a different plane and wondered why. She looked up. Her glance met his. Then she understood. He wasn't holding back anymore.

Happiness surged through her. Slowly she began to show him how she felt. With deliberate slowness, she kissed his chin, his neck, then nipped the ends of his fingers with her teeth.

Pulling her toward him, he licked a line along the column of her throat and around her nipples. When he let out a deep chuckle, ripples ran up her spine. Obviously he liked her new sense of freedom, too.

"Ahh. What you do to me is unreal." He pressed her tightly to him, rubbing his erection against her belly.

"Feels real to me."

"Let me show you just how real it is."

With that, he rolled on top of her. His eyes glinted in the subdued lighting of the apartment. Slowly he entered her, then pulled back, then in. Teasing her. Until she couldn't take it anymore:

"You're cruel," she whispered.

"Just taking my time."

"I know. I love it. But I hate it. Oh . . . never mind."

She met his gaze. Love looked back at her.

He moved faster, thrust harder. When she couldn't stand any more, he stiffened against her and let out a cry. She pulled his body tighter, deeper into herself, wanting to feel every part of him. Together they crashed through, and collapsed against each other.

Later, when they'd caught their breath, he propped himself up on one elbow and gazed at her. "This keeps getting better and better."

"No kidding. You just graduated from novice to expert."

"Think so, huh?"

"I *know* so," she said.

"I wondered if I'd ever get to hold you again. Or touch you like this."

As she watched pain move across the face she'd come to love, it hit her again how close they'd come to losing each other. "I kept telling myself I had to accept it was over," she said. "That you didn't want me."

He asked, "Still think that?"

"Hardly."

He looked down at himself, then raised one eyebrow. "Not yet, but give me a few minutes."

"You've got all the time you want." She paused, then asked, "This is going to work out, isn't it?"

"Absolutely. Why do you ask?"

"Maybe it's silly, but you never actually said you wanted to make a commitment. Are you really sure you're ready?"

"Let me put your mind at rest." He brushed his thumb across her lips. "If I'd met you first, second, or last, I'd love you. And only you." Grabbing her, he rolled over and over with her on the big bed, miscalculated, and sent them both tumbling over the edge onto her Berber rug.

"Ouch," she said. "Could you maybe love me a little less and pay attention to your sense of direction a little more?"

"I'm deeply wounded." His smile slipped a notch. "You know, you haven't told me that you love me."

Her heart threatened to burst. There was something about having a man as powerful as Jack need her that ranked up there with the best aphrodisiacs. "Oh, I do love you. I've never felt this way before." After planting a lingering kiss on each temple, then on his firm, sexy lips, she added, "I want to get to know your demons on a first-name basis. And I won't push you away. Promise."

"I'll hold you to that." He pulled her fiercely against him. "Are you ready for a new challenge?"

"Such as?"

"Spending our lives together."

"Are you asking me to marry you?" She playfully swatted his shoulder.

"Sweetheart, I may have decided not to become a priest, but surely you don't expect me to live in sin. . . ."

"But where are my flowers, the ring, the organ grinder?"

"Organ grinder?" He clutched his privates.

"Stop already. You know what I mean. Where's the pomp and circumstance?" She put her hand on her forehead in mock anguish. "I want flowers!"

"Sweetheart, I'll cover you in rose petals, pour champagne in your shoes, dance a fandango on your dining room table. Whatever it takes."

She batted her eyes. "This is all so sudden."

"I've got it all planned." He scooted next to her, excited about the thought of making a life together. "We can get married at St. Evangeline's Church. Father Quinn runs it. He's a friend of mine—you'll like him." He began to peel back the sheet that she clutched to her breasts. "And we'll invite the kids from the shelter."

"Right, Lamar can be ring bearer." She let out a purr when his mouth connected with the tender skin of her belly. "But let's keep Pam away from the votive candles, okay?"

"Good thinking."

"And Nathan can give me away."

He glanced up at her. "How about your parents? I'd like to meet them."

She thought for a moment. "Yeah, maybe it's time to bring them back in my life." She gasped when his lips found an especially sensitive spot. "But I can't think of my parents at a time like this; it's indecent."

"No, there's nothing indecent about this." He ran his hand along the silky skin of her thigh. Delicious. "I know a great inn we can stay at in the wine country for our honeymoon."

"Oh, yes!"

"Like the way that sounds?"

"No, the way that feels," she murmured, wrapping her arms around him. "We'll plan later. Don't you have business to take care of first?"

"Oh, I wouldn't call this business." He looked into her dark, loving eyes.

"What would you call it?"

"Heaven on earth." He paused. "Kiss me, would you?"

She joyfully obliged.